Cassidy's Cowboy

Cassidy's Cowboy

Search for Love Series

KAREN ROSE SMITH

Note From The Author

I wrote about a heroine in CASSIDY'S COWBOY who has dyslexia, a developmental reading disorder. I've researched the subject, but I'm not an expert. This novel isn't about the condition itself, but rather the effects of it. The inability to decipher the written word is a subject we don't discuss much. But reading is such an essential part of life that I decided to explore the issue in this novel. As an author and a former teacher, it's important to me.

I had experience with dyslexia when I taught second grade. The disability concerns the part of the brain that decodes symbols. I believe teachers are more aware these days than even a dozen years ago and reading problems are caught sooner. Early intervention is paramount. But children have slipped through the cracks for many years. In my case, as a teacher, the learning disability manifested in my students with behavioral problems. When a child feels he or she can't keep up with peers, when a child feels he or she is on the outside looking in, if this child feels unable to learn, behavior changes. Acting out is common. So is sullenness or withdrawal. A teacher working with parents tries to find the root of the problem. Now testing can aid in this cause.

My heroine had a reading disability that was never diagnosed. Her history in foster care helped her slip through the cracks until teachers and caregivers just considered her a difficult child. Fortunately she found a mentor who took her under her wing. But instead of addressing the problem, she helped Cassidy live with it. Was she an enabler or a loved one helping Cassidy cope? Because she finally had people around her who cared, Cassidy learned tricks to hide her reading disability from those outside her circle. She had a great memory. In the same way a child memorizes a favorite book, Cassidy used her memory to retain information and absorb it. She learned to duck situations that could reveal what she felt was a flaw. Imagine the vigilance necessary to remember everything—signs, instructions, the meaning of symbols. Anxiety can become a huge by-product in fearing the secret of being unable to read will be identified. However, in the end, Cassidy has to reveal her secret to the person she cares about most.

Unconditional love teamed with a dose of reality wins the day in Cassidy's story. I wish all of our children could be so fortunate. May reading always bring you escape, pleasure, knowledge and new discoveries.

All my best,
Karen Rose Smith

Cassidy's Cowboy

Chapter One

"Did you ever think about looking for our dad?" Cassidy Sullivan snipped roses from the bush along the side of the house and handed them to her twin sister, Lucy, to put in the basket that swung from her arm.

Complete silence met Cassie's question as she turned to see if her sister had heard her. She'd said it in a low voice, a thought that had been reverberating in her own head since Lucy had found her six months ago.

Early summer in Wyoming was an awakening time for the wildflowers, the honeysuckle and the roses. She loved Twin Pines Ranch, an inheritance from the mentor who'd saved her from taking the wrong life road. But she loved her new-found sister even more, although she was still keeping a secret from her, a secret she'd soon have to reveal. Lucy was as perceptive as her new husband, Zack, and he'd figured it out the first time he'd met Cassie.

"How would we ever do that?" Lucy finally responded. "We knew very little about our mother, let alone our father."

Cassie knew at times Lucy might still feel hurt that their mother had given her up for adoption, yet kept Cassie until the day she'd died. At twenty-six they both had their own lives now, but their childhoods still had power over them.

Cassie clipped a few magenta rose stems, careful of the thorns, then said, "Let's go into the house. I want to show you something."

The large ranch house on Twin Pines Ranch was three stories, covered with Wedgwood blue siding and accented by a wraparound apron veranda. Caned rocking chairs waited there for visitors over the summer. There were three bedrooms on the second floor, and the attic, used for storage, was hot and musty.

As the women ran up the steps to the front porch, Lucy asked, "Do you think the men will be out all morning mending fence?"

"Do you miss Zack already?" Cassie teased, knowing Zack and her twin were very much newlyweds and not apart any more than they had to be.

"Sure, I miss him," Lucy said with a bit of a shy smile. "Life's a little crazy right now with living in town so he can start his practice, and going out to Mom and Dad's as much as we can to check out the site where the house is being built. It's going to be so great, being able to be alone with Zack and being on the ranch."

"From what he said, he feels the same way. So he's joining an established physician's practice in Long Brush?"

"Yes. It will be easier this way on everyone. The docs can cover for each other on weekends. That's how we came this weekend. Dr. Brewster is covering for him."

"It sounds as if you've combined the best of both worlds. Zack certainly seems happy. I think he's finally dropped the weight of everything that happened to him back in California. And is Marty staying with the program?" Lucy's adopted brother Marty had become an alcoholic. Largely through Zack's efforts, he'd gone through rehab.

"Seems to be. Our church has AA meetings once a week and he attends those. Other times he'll call his sponsor or he'll drive to Long Brush to another meeting. He understands the one day at a time philosophy and he's trying to make amends."

Cassie understood how a problem could turn into a lifelong battle. "When you take a wrong turn, or you go off the wrong road, I think you do the most damage to yourself, at least if you're single. I know I did. Once you get over the humiliation and you can find a little confidence again, that helps everything else."

"Maybe you and Marty should talk."

"We did at Christmas."

Cassie didn't understand a lot about marriage and families. Shifted from one foster home to the next from the time she was five, she hadn't known stability until Tina Christopher had taken her in when she was seventeen. Tina had been a widow then, so Cassie had never seen what a good marriage was supposed to be.

"How's Zack handling being part of a large family?"

"He grumps once in a while because he thinks he knows best, but eventually he comes around to see what any of us really need, whether that's a pat on the head or a swift kick."

Cassie laughed. "I can see Zack doing both. He's so great with the horses. I wish I could use him to train the new hand I've hired. Clem tries too hard, wants to be too aggressive. He definitely doesn't understand patience like Zack does."

"How old is he?"

"Just out of high school with nowhere else to go. So I told him I'd give him a chance."

"Are you a sucker for a sad story?"

"Heck, I can be a sucker for any story. Though I don't cry my eyes out like you do watching one of those card commercials on TV."

This time Lucy laughed.

They entered the living room, then went straight to the kitchen. Cassie had readied two Waterford vases. "Tina loved having these vases full of flowers this time of year. I miss her most then. I keep them filled with flowers all summer."

"That's a way to remember her well."

Cassie hesitated, then went on. "I still haven't found a way to do that with our mom. After she died, I tried to forget, not remember, because it hurt too much.

"And now?" Lucy asked with so much compassion Cassie wanted to hug her.

"Now—"

Lucy set the wicker basket on the counter and Cassie said, "We can arrange these later. Come on, let's go up to my room."

At the top of the stairs, the first door on the left was Cassie's. It wasn't much bigger than the others, but it did have a private bath. It had been Tina's room, and Cassie hadn't changed much here since her mentor had died, though she had redecorated in the past five years—the guest bedrooms, the living room, new wallpaper in the kitchen. She'd changed those rooms because memories of her life with Tina were alive there...and they hurt. The changes reminded her to think ahead rather than back. But in this room, she remembered Tina. She even still had a few of her clothes hanging in the closet. Silly, maybe, but she liked to take a whiff of Tina's riding coat. She liked to see those tall boots standing in the corner. It made her feel closer.

Cassie went to the dresser and pulled out the top drawer. Lucy crossed to her and they stared at each other in the mirror. They were identical twins in most ways. Zack had pointed out a few differences. Cassie's hair was darker brown and Lucy had a dimple on the right side of her cheek when she smiled. But they really were mirror images.

After Cassie opened the second drawer in the cherry wood dresser, she reached deep inside to the back and pulled out a suede pouch. It was easy to see it was old. The suede was worn around the edges and the leather ties were scraped from drawing the pouch closed. She held it in her hand as if it were her most precious possession. And maybe it was.

"My mom and I didn't have much, and I don't remember a lot. But I do remember many nights we split a dinner she brought home from the restaurant where she waitressed. I think I told you we lived in a one-room apartment. She slept on the sofa and I slept on pillows on the floor."

Her voice caught as some of the faded memories took on a little more color again. After a moment, she went on. "Even when I was five, I knew we didn't have anything valuable, anything worth keeping, except—" She looked down at the pouch. "For this. Whenever we'd leave the apartment, Mom stuffed it in a sock and then pushed that sock into a cookie jar. But while we were there she'd take it out and lay it on top of the orange crate where she kept a couple of books. Sometimes she'd just pick it up and hold it and stare at it in such a way that made me not want to ask any questions."

Cassie opened the pouch and slid a gold pocket watch into her palm. "One day I did ask her what it was, and she told me it was a watch and it had belonged to somebody very special. That's all she'd ever say. The night she was killed, she went out and a neighbor came over to stay with me. We were watching TV when the police came to the door. I heard everything. I don't think I understood everything. They said my mom was dead. It was dark and she walked across the middle of the street and a car hit her. He told the neighbor somebody would be coming for me. Flo told me to get my favorite toy because I'd need it...that I wouldn't be coming back. So I got my stuffed horse, and when everyone else was talking, I went to the cookie jar and pulled out the sock. The horse had a tear in the middle, so I just stuffed the sock in his stomach. No matter where I went or who had me, I protected that horse. When I got a little older I sewed him up. But I've always wondered about this." She handed the watch to Lucy.

A few times since Cassie had met Lucy, they'd look at each other and known what the other was thinking. That was definitely true of this moment.

But Cassie needed to put it into words. "You found me with only a picture, a birth date and a last name."

"Gillian found you."

"Yes, I know. She finds missing persons and she's obviously very good. Before you found me, before you told me how Gillian did it, I never would have believed in a— a psychic. But I thought maybe since she uses objects to pick up sensations, that maybe, just maybe, she'd see something that would help us know who this belonged to. Maybe it wasn't our father. Maybe it was a grandfather. Maybe it was another special man our mom had met. I don't know. And I don't know if it's worth bothering Gillian about, or if she'd have time to do this for us. But ever since you found me, I've been thinking about it and I knew I had to ask you what you thought."

Lucy closed the watch and ran her thumb over the top of the scroll engraving in the gold. "We need to think about it."

Cassie felt a little deflated. After all, this was the reason she hadn't brought it up before. Maybe Lucy would want no part of finding out who their dad had been—a dad who had left them or maybe just another man who had been in and out of their mother's life.

But then Lucy went on. "I waited a while before I decided to try to find you. I found out a little bit of information, couldn't go any farther, and that's when Zack recommended Gillian. But before I decided to go ahead with finding you, my biggest fear was that you wouldn't want to see me, that you wouldn't want to have any part of me. And I think that's even more true and more of a fear when trying to find a parent. If this did belong to our father, what did our mother mean to him? Did he mean more to her than she meant to him? Would he have a family now? And if he has a family, would they want us to be part of it? Would he want us to be part of it? Do you see what I mean?"

Cassie wasn't any more open to getting hurt than Lucy, maybe even less so. Lucy had grown up with the McIntyres, a loving, adopted family who had given her a sense of self-worth and a confidence to find what she was good at and pursue a dream. Until Cassie was seventeen, no one had wanted to give to her, they'd only wanted to take from her and use her. She didn't trust easily. She didn't make friends easily. She certainly didn't wear her heart on her sleeve. So she understood everything Lucy was saying and realized it wasn't a rejection of her idea at all, it was just a pause for them to think and not be reckless, to think instead of getting hurt. After all, they were twins and together in this.

"You're right," she said. "We should think about it."

Lucy looked relieved. "We can talk to Zack, too, and see what he thinks. You know I trust his advice. But that's up to you."

Cassie was beginning to trust Zack, too. After all, he'd kept her secret so far. And that had to be hard, being a newlywed and wanting to share everything with Lucy. Yet he was also a doctor and knew about doctor-patient confidentiality. She had a feeling he was looking at her secret somewhat like that. Still she didn't want it to go long.

She didn't want her secret to cause a rift between Zack and Lucy. "I need to tell you something."

"Something Zack already knows?"

Cassie felt sideswiped. "Why do you think that?"

"The first time we came to visit you here, I knew the two of you shared something. When we returned to the Rising Star, I asked Zack if he was attracted to you because I misread the signals. Zack told me he wasn't attracted to you, he was attracted to me. He told me you were just talking and I knew that's all it had been. But since then, when you've come to visit us, or we've come here, I can sense something between the two of you and I think you confided in him."

Now Cassie was sure she had to tell Lucy what she'd kept from everyone except Tina and her foreman Loren all these years. "I've kept a secret all my life, Lucy. Zack figured it out. I didn't tell you because...because it makes me feel so inferior. It makes me feel humiliated sometimes."

Lucy put her hand on her sister's shoulder. "You can tell me anything, absolutely anything."

Cassie took a deep breath, then let it out. "I can't read."

Cassie didn't see the shock she expected in Lucy's eyes. She didn't see judgment or even pity which would have made Cassie run in the opposite direction. She only saw compassion as Lucy murmured, "That must be so difficult for you."

"I've learned to cope," Cassie confessed. "I think I have something called dyslexia, though I've never been diagnosed. Loren's the only one who knew for a long time. I mean, Tina did, too. And Rachel knows now. They looked it up on the computer. I mix up my letters. I see them differently on the page. That's why I cut school so much, why I got into trouble. Once Tina brought me here I didn't need to know how to read. The horses and I communicate just fine. I can ride a fence line and cut cattle and muck out stalls without reading."

"But how do you run the ranch?"

"Well, the thing is, once I hear something I usually remember it. Rachel takes care of the household necessities. Loren does all the numbers and forms on the computer. But he reads me everything. I take it in and use it when I need to." She didn't know how she would handle it without her foreman and her housekeeper.

"Oh, Cassie." Lucy wrapped her arms around her sister and Cassie didn't think she'd ever felt more loved. Tears sprang to her eyes and she swiped them away. "Zack saw I didn't have any reading material around, that I had X's on the calendar so I could count the days."

"Here I thought you were just neat."

Cassie laughed.

Suddenly outside there was the sound of horses clopping into the corral and men's voices. "I guess they're back. We'd better go down and fix lunch. Rachel went into town to pick up extra supplies."

"Not for us, I hope," Lucy said. "We'll be leaving after breakfast tomorrow."

"No. Although Zack probably could eat me out of house and home. They're for guests coming next week."

"Guests?"

"Loren's nephew from Vermont, Ben, is coming with his daughter, Julie. His wife left him and his daughter over a year ago and Julie is having a hard time of it. I think she's nine. So with school out, Loren suggested they come and stay here for a few weeks. They'll be living in the guest cabin but will come up here for meals." Over the years she'd seen pictures of Ben. He had wavy black hair, green eyes and a few years ago, a smile that had made her wonder what he'd really be like if she met him in person.

"You won't mind having them around?"

"I doubt it. It won't interfere with my routine. As good as Loren has been to me, I couldn't say no to anything he wanted. I talked to Ben last week and he seems like an okay guy." Actually, his deep voice and his concern for his daughter had resonated inside her in a big way. Especially when she remembered that smile.

Shoving those thoughts aside, she went on, "He spent summers on Twin Pines with Loren when he was a kid. But he hasn't been back here in a dozen years or more. Now he's the CEO of his own carpet company. But the main thing is, he's concerned about his daughter, and I can respect that. Anything to help a little girl heal. I know what it's like."

A low growl of thunder began and Cassie crossed to the window. "Boy, that was quick. It looks like storms are rolling in."

"It's that time of year," Lucy said. She walked over

to the window, stood beside Cassie and then handed her the watch. "We'll know when the time is right to do this. If you suddenly feel strongly about it, call me. If I suddenly feel strongly about it, I'll call you. Deal?"

"Deal," Cassie agreed, as she wrapped her arm around her sister's shoulders and wondered if either of them were ready to invite a new storm into their lives.

Chapter Two

Ben O'Donnell, his daughter's hand in his, walked beside his uncle as they headed for the guest cabin on Twin Pines Ranch. He and Julie had just arrived when his uncle had come to greet them, to take them to meet Cassidy Sullivan.

It seemed odd that he hadn't been back here for years. But his uncle had always come east to visit on holidays...or in between. And as Ben had gone to college, graduated, started his own company and gotten married, travel west hadn't been on his agenda.

Now, however, he and Julie needed a change of scene. And not just any change. Over the past year, Julie's schoolwork had suffered and she'd become withdrawn. He couldn't make up for her mother abandoning her eighteen months ago, but as the therapist had encouraged, he could help her learn to be happy again. Maybe they could both learn to be happy. He didn't care so much for himself. After all, he had his company. But Julie...she needed something he and Vermont couldn't give her.

"Things have changed a bit since I last talked to you," his uncle Loren said. "Storms went through here, uprooting trees, tearing things apart. So you won't be staying in the guest cabin, you'll be staying up at the house."

Ben stopped. "With Miss Sullivan?"

Loren turned to him. "Don't say it like she's a rattlesnake that could get into your boots while you're sleeping. There's plenty of room. After all, I can vouch for your character."

Julie squeezed his hand and he knew she was uncertain about being here, in a strange place. Since her mom left, she'd been uncertain about everything. If staying here didn't go well, they could fly back to Vermont and try something else, though he wasn't sure what.

Loren's appraising gaze scanned him from eyes to shoes. "You're going to have to get rid of those fancy duds and get some rough-and-tumble gear."

Ben felt himself becoming defensive, even though he'd always known his uncle was plain speaking and honest to a fault. The fancy clothes he spoke of consisted of a tan, oxford shirt, khakis and leather loafers. "I have jeans in my suitcase."

"Well, good. I hope you've got boots in there, too, because you're going to need them."

Need them for what? Ben wondered. After all, he'd thought of this as kind of a vacation. He hadn't actually considered being part of a working ranch. He'd tried to insist on paying Cassidy Sullivan for their stay here. But she'd been adamantly against it. He'd found her as determined as his uncle! Well, Ben could be that way, too. He'd repay her somehow.

Whenever she spoke of his uncle, she did so with a downright fondness in her voice. He supposed she'd depended on his Uncle Loren a lot, since Tina Christopher had died. How difficult would it be for a woman not even thirty to run a ranch this size on her own?

When they came in sight of the guest cabin, Ben almost stopped again. "Did you have a tornado go through here?"

There were two uprooted trees and shingles scattered on the ground.

"We've had a series of storms over the past week, drenching rain again last night. That's why Cassie's down here this morning. She insisted she didn't want to pull any men away from their ranch duties. She can be one stubborn woman sometimes."

Ben knew all about stubborn women. If Melinda hadn't been so stubborn, they'd still be married. Or would they? He'd lived with his if-onlys and what-ifs for the past eighteen months. That hadn't done him or Julie any good. But he didn't know how to move past the guilt and regrets. Maybe instead of working out in the gym he needed to ride a horse, split logs, feel the sun on his back. Maybe he could shove work into the backseat while he was here. He doubted it, but he could try.

Julie held on even more tightly to his hand as they approached the door of the small cabin and country music spilled out. He teasingly flipped one of her braids. If anyone had told him before Melinda left that he could learn how to braid hair, tie bows on the ends and have a tea party with his daughter, he would have told them they were crazy. But a man did what a man had to do. A father did what a father had to do.

When Ben first caught sight of Cassidy Sullivan, she was pushing a large overstuffed chair from one side of the cabin to the other. Apparently she'd been moving furniture for a while, because everything from the one side of the cabin was on the other side. He noticed the large, wet spot on the floor and the buckets half-filled with what he supposed was rain water. When he looked up at the ceiling, he spotted where it had come from. There was a gaping hole where the roof had been torn off.

Because music blared from a radio, she hadn't heard them approach.

Loren called over the music. "Cassie!"

She turned to face them.

Ben was struck immediately by the look of dogged determination on her face and then the affection in her brown eyes as she gave her attention to his uncle. When she crossed the room to turn down the radio, he saw she moved gracefully and had a figure that—

Her tight jeans and T-shirt initiated a startling response in his body, one he hadn't experienced for well over a year and a half. To cover his reaction to her, Ben quipped, "Looks like you need another hand more than you need a house guest."

She crossed to him and extended her hand. "It's good to meet you, Mr. O'Donnell."

"Ben," he said, without thinking why that had come to his lips so quickly.

"Ben," she said, with a nod that told him she wouldn't soon forget.

Her hand in his felt small and fragile. He found himself wanting to hold on a little longer to feel the calluses, to tell her she shouldn't work so hard. From what his uncle had said and what he had seen so far, she did.

Her cheeks flushed a little as she pulled her hand from his, and he wondered if she'd felt that sting of awareness, too. An awareness that was almost as foreign to him as his daughter's laughter.

Cassie crouched down in front of Julie. "Hi, there. My name's Cassie. What's yours?"

Julie looked up to her dad as if seeking approval. He nodded. "Julie," she said.

Cassie's smile widened. "It's good to meet you, Julie. Do you like horses?"

His daughter shrugged and looked down at her sneakers. "I don't know. I've never touched one."

"Maybe we can do something about that while you're here. Would you like to go up to the house and see your room?"

Again Julie shrugged.

But Cassie didn't give up. She said, "You can pick the one you want."

Julie suddenly looked interested. "I can?"

"Yep. I'll leave this mess for a little while and get you settled in."

When Cassie rose to her feet, Julie looked up at her with interest and her hand didn't quite hold on so tightly to Ben's.

Fifteen minutes later after Cassie had introduced them to Rachel Mayer, Cassie's housekeeper, Ben had taken their gear from the rented SUV and carried it upstairs. As Cassie led Julie from room to room, the little girl studied one with pin-striped blue-and-white wallpaper and small pink roses. A second was more sedate with wine-and-navy striped paper. Julie surveyed the room with the blue-and-white striped wallpaper from the doorway. Lace curtains at the windows blew in the June breeze. The many throw pillows on the white chenille spread were inviting.

"I like this one," Julie decided. "Which one is yours, Daddy?"

He pointed to the one right next door with the wine-and-navy wallpaper. "I think this one will do just fine. And I'm within shouting distance if you need me."

Cassie gave him a speculative look but he didn't explain about his daughter's bad dreams. Time enough for that if they occurred here.

"So, how about some dinner?" Cassie asked. "Rachel should have it almost ready. You'll have to tell her what you like so she can make your favorite things."

"If it was up to Julie, she'd eat burgers and fries every night."

"You like 'em, too," his daughter pointed out, and he was glad to hear some spirit in her voice. That had been missing for so long.

"Yes, I do. But we'll have to come up with some other food for Miss Rachel to make. Put your thinking cap on."

She gave him one of those Oh-Daddy smiles. "I don't have a thinking cap."

A short time later, Rachel served them dinner and sat down with them to eat. Loren joined them too, and

Ben watched the interaction between his uncle and Rachel, who was a little younger than him. It wasn't what they said, but the looks they exchanged, and Ben wondered if his uncle had been holding out on him, if maybe there was a romantic interest in his life.

Searching for a way to keep the dinner conversation going, Ben asked Cassie, "So you grew up around here?"

A hush settled over the table. Rachel, Loren and Cassie exchanged looks and he wondered what that was about. But Cassie answered, "I came to live with Tina when I was seventeen. She taught me everything I know about horses and how to handle them, how to run cattle—"

Loren interrupted. "How to keep us all under your thumb."

Cassie laughed. "I suppose, she did. But I soon figured out if I treated my hands with respect, they'd treat me the same."

As Rachel rose to her feet and began to clear dishes, she asked Julie, "What would you like for breakfast? Eggs, pancakes, toast, cereal? I have a little bit of everything."

While Julie discussed breakfast with Cassie's housekeeper, Ben wondered why Rachel and Loren were so protective of Cassie...he wondered what she was hiding.

After the table was cleared, Ben and Julie changed into jeans and T-shirts, slipped on their jackets, went downstairs and outside. They spotted Cassie in a corral where a golden mare was running in circles.

"She's pretty," Julie said, almost in awe as they approached the fence. But Ben was looking at Cassie, not the horse and Julie's words rang way too true. Cassie Sullivan was pretty...and curvy.

He heard Loren say to her, "I haven't been able to get anywhere near her today without her bucking, stomping and rearing. Be careful."

"She's not scared of me," Cassie assured him. "I'll be fine."

Ben could feel Loren's concern as Cassie took a few steps closer to the agitated horse. He wanted to rush in there himself and pull her out.

Julie tugged on his hand. "What's she gonna do?"

He didn't know if his daughter meant Cassie or the horse, but he said in an even tone, "Let's wait and see."

He hoped he wasn't witnessing a disaster in the making, because that was the last thing Julie needed. But before he could scoop his daughter up and take her back to the house, Cassie took one slow step at a time toward the golden horse.

The horse blew out breath and whinnied, swished its tail and took a few steps to the side.

Cassie just faced her squarely, gazing at her. It was as if some silent communication passed between them. The horse stood perfectly still and so did Cassie.

Then he heard Cassie say in a low voice, "Good girl. You're fine. You're really going to like it here, I promise you. I'll be back to visit you tomorrow."

She didn't try to touch the horse but slowly backed away, the same way she'd walked in. She slipped through the gate and closed it.

Ben let out a breath he didn't even know he was holding.

"She talked to her," Julie said.

"Yes, she did, and I think the horse heard her. Maybe we can find out the horse's name."

Julie let go of his hand as they walked up to the corral.

"What was that about?" he asked.

"She's a wild mustang," Cassie explained. "I adopted her. The Bureau of Land Management thins the herds and they send horses all over the country for adoption. This mare came from the Big Horns. Her name's Sunny. Isn't she beautiful?"

"I haven't been around horses for a while," Ben said. "For a horse she's all right."

Loren chuckled.

When Ben's gaze met Cassie's, he couldn't seem to look away. But he finally did, feeling disconcerted.

As if Cassie had felt the same magnetic pull and was unnerved, too, she turned toward the house. "We're usually up before dawn, so I'm going to say goodnight. I'll see you all in the morning." To Julie she said, "Maybe I can show you some of our tamer horses tomorrow. Their noses are as soft as velvet."

"Can I touch one?"

"Better than that, you might even be able to ride one. Your dad and I will talk about it."

Before Ben could protest, or even say goodnight, Cassie was on the way up to the house, out of earshot.

Ben looked after her, intrigued by her. Melinda had been petite, poised, sophisticated, and always vigilant about them moving in the right circles. Ben didn't know Cassie's background, but already he suspected she was down-to-earth, practical, with her feet always on the ground.

He said to Loren, "What's her story?"

"How do you know she has one?"

"Everybody has a story," Ben responded, knowing it was true.

"Cassie's is a little different than most. It's hers to tell. Maybe if you get to know her, she will."

Get to know her. Did he want to do that? After all, he and Julie would be here a few weeks and then they'd be gone.

Maybe exchanging stories wasn't such a great idea.

In her room, Cassie turned the pages of the decorating magazine. She loved to decorate. Everyone who saw the rooms she'd done told her she had an eye for color. Last fall, she'd even helped a neighbor redo her living room. Cassie couldn't read the descriptions of the rooms in the pictures, but she could absorb every detail of the way they were designed. The thing was, tonight that couldn't keep her occupied and she felt downright trapped. She'd stayed in her room while she'd heard Ben and Julie getting ready for bed. She hadn't wanted to interrupt their nighttime routine. But now all was quiet.

Ben.

She felt something when she looked at him, something unusual. She was used to working with men, for goodness sakes. But none of them had ever made her stomach tumble a little. None of them had ever made her feel a bit...tingly. She knew the kind of man Ben was. At thirty-seven, he was CEO of his own company and he was used to fine things. She could tell from his clothes and the suitcases he'd brought in. And she suspected he was used to women who were polished, and who could certainly read. If he knew she would have ended up in juvenile hall instead of with Tina would he let her anywhere near Julie? She didn't know.

Maybe one of Rachel's chocolate chip cookies and a glass of milk could settle her down. Morning would come long before she wanted it to at this rate.

Fifteen minutes later, she'd gone downstairs and was coming back up with two cookies on a napkin and a glass of milk when the door to Ben's room opened. As she mounted the last three steps, she saw he was shirtless, wearing only a pair of jeans that hung low on his hips. In fact, she could follow all of that curly black chest hair down below his navel.

Her gaze snapped up to his face. "I just went downstairs for a snack," she said. Rattled, she asked, "Want a cookie?"

A slow smile slipped across his lips and that same tummy-twirling sensation happened again. "Sure," he said, coming closer.

He was close enough to touch and she felt more flustered than she could ever remember feeling. "I hope I didn't wake you," she murmured.

"I'm a light sleeper. I heard a noise and thought Julie might be up. I just wanted to make sure she was okay."

Cassie had slung on her robe—a pink cotton one—but she could feel the belt becoming undone and she only had a silky nightgown underneath. "I hope you don't mind, but Loren told me about your wife leaving."

Ben hadn't spoken of his personal life at all and she couldn't blame him for wanting to keep it private. But being around Julie, she needed to know what had happened so she didn't say something stupid. "I want to make sure I handle Julie the right way. I don't want to say anything that would hurt her."

Ben's mouth had tightened at the mention of his marriage, or rather the end of it, but then at the mention of Julie his expression softened again. "Melinda left eighteen months ago. She decided she didn't want to be married anymore, that she wanted to accept a job her cosmetics company offered her in Seattle."

"And she didn't want to take Julie with her?"

"No, she didn't."

Cassie couldn't understand a woman who could just walk away from her child. Yes, her mother had given up Lucy, but that had been because she couldn't take care of her. This was altogether different. "Does Julie see her?"

"The truth is, she didn't see much of either of us before Melinda left. We had a nanny. We both had careers and we thought she was okay. But then after Melinda left she wasn't okay. She saw her at Christmas at Melinda's place in Seattle. I thought of taking Julie to see her this summer, but Melinda's in Europe right now. She's living the life she always wanted to live. I don't understand it any more than Julie did."

"I'm sorry."

He gave a nonchalant shrug. "I'll get over it, but I don't think Julie ever will."

"I lost my mom when I was five," Cassie said before she thought better of it. "I never knew my dad."

"Is that when you came here? Tina adopted you?"

"No, it's a long story. But the good news is, last fall I learned I had a twin sister. Lucy and I are thinking about searching for our dad, but I'm not sure if that will happen or not."

"A twin," Ben said. "How great is that! I always hoped Julie wouldn't be an only child." He stopped abruptly, recovering from whatever he was thinking. He asked, "So do you feel connected to your sister in a special way? Or is that a myth?"

"Lucy and I are practically identical, and since her first call to me, yes, I do feel connected. But not in some mystical way."

She wasn't going to go into how Lucy had found her. That would be putting a royal strain on this conversation.

Her belt suddenly gave way and her robe opened. Ben's gaze drifted to her breasts and for a moment the world seemed to stop turning.

But then he gave her a crooked smile and brought his gaze back up to her face. "Are you still willing to give up one of those cookies?"

Thank goodness the man had panache and a sense of humor. "Sure." He took one from the napkin and she turned to go into her room.

But then they both heard a cry. Julie called, "Daddy!"

Ben dropped the cookie to the floor and raced to

his daughter's bedside with Cassie following. She really should stay out of this. Yes, she should.

But the little girl's cry had torn through her heart and she simply couldn't.

Chapter Three

B en had scooped Julie into his arms and was rocking her. His daughter was still crying and his face was filled with all the anguish he felt for her.

He kept murmuring to her, "It's okay, baby. I'm right here. I'm never going to leave."

Cassie felt for the two of them. But this tableau was too private for her to be a part of. How many times in her life had she felt scared? That everyone she'd loved had left? She was so glad Julie had her dad.

A dad. Cassie caught Ben's eye and in a low voice asked, "Do you need anything?"

He just shook his head.

Moments later, she left father and daughter alone, went into the hall and picked up the broken cookie, gathering the crumbs. Pensively, she went into her room, dumped the cookie into the waste can, picked up her cell phone and pressed speed dial for Lucy.

Yes, it was late, but they called each other anytime day or night. That was the wonderful thing about having a twin.

Lucy answered, sounding a bit foggy. "Cassie? Is everything okay?"

"I'm sorry if I woke you."

"It's okay. You know that. What's up?"

"Have you thought about trying to find our dad?"

"Yes, I have. I talked to Zack about it, too. He said if we can find another missing piece of who we are, we should go for it."

"And what do you think?

"I think finding you was one of the best things that ever happened to me and no matter how it would turn out, with trying to find our father, we should try. Then we could say we did."

Cassie laughed. "Now that's a philosophy if I ever heard one. But I like it. Will you call Gillian?"

"First thing in the morning. And I'll let you know what she says. Do you want to tell me what motivated this call?"

"Not right now. Maybe later."

Lucy didn't ask any more questions and that was one of the things Cassie loved about her sister. Lucy accepted her the way she was. "Good-night, Sis."

"Good-night, Luce. Sweet dreams."

After Cassie ended the call, she felt compelled to check on Ben and Julie again. The door to the room was still wide open. He'd pulled the wing chair next to his daughter's bed and was sitting there. Cassie could see that Julie had fallen back to sleep.

When Ben spotted Cassie, he rose from the chair and came to the doorway.

"Does this happen often?" Cassie asked.

"It's better now than it was after Melinda left. Now it's only every couple of weeks. In the beginning I spent most nights by her bed. She's afraid I'm going to leave, too. I don't know how to reassure her I won't. Melinda broke her trust and does nothing to reassure her that she's still her mom and that she loves her. Sometimes I get so angry."

Ben's hands were balled into fists and she could see the fury in his eyes. How hard it must be to deal with his ex-wife and to do what was best for his daughter every time.

Understanding, she said, "But you can't express it. You have to smooth the waters and hope for the best."

He seemed surprised that she could sympathize with him. But she remembered all those years in foster families where she did just that—tried to smooth the waters and get along, get through it, hope for a better day. She'd had better days, and she hoped Ben and Julie would, too.

"Are you going to be able to sleep in that chair?" she asked.

"Sleep's not the priority. Julie's sense of security is."

"You know, it might be easier for both of you if you had some help trying to make her feel secure. If there's anything Loren or I can do—"

He shook his head. "Julie has to realize deep down in her heart that she can always count on me. I can't trust anyone else not to let her down."

It was easy to see that Ben had built defenses around his heart since his wife had left. He was the type of man who knew what he wanted and knew what he had to do. Nothing would get in the way of that.

As they stood there, him bare-chested, her in a nightgown and robe, awareness seemed to sweep across the two of them—that man-woman awareness that brings with it sexual tension and a crackling electricity Cassie had rarely felt before.

Gazing into Ben's very green eyes, she felt attraction that was strong and body-shaking. He was so much taller than she was, a good six inches. His shoulders were broad, his arms muscled. His gaze dropped to her lips and she knew what he was thinking because she was thinking the same thing. What would his lips on hers feel like? How would she feel with his strong arms around her?

Her heart pounded faster, and for an instant she thought they both leaned a little closer to each other. But then he straightened and she took a step back. She was not about to get involved with a man who had expectations and standards that she could never meet.

Getting a grip on her imagination and her thoughts, she focused on his daughter again. "If you need anything, don't hesitate to come get me. I'll see you in the morning."

"Good-night, Cassie."

It was the first he'd used her name and for some reason his use of it seemed very intimate. She didn't dwell on that idea very long.

Crossing to her room, she shut the door behind her, trying also to shut out hope and dreams that could only be dashed by reality.

After breakfast the following morning, Julie surprised them all by asking Cassie, "Can we go see Sunny?"

Cassie had watched the little girl eat breakfast quietly while she and Loren and Ben and Rachel talked about the ranch and what had to be done.

Ben had insisted, "I'd like to help out. I need to keep in shape while I'm here and that's one way to do it."

Loren had said, "You always were a good rider."

That's when Julie had asked Cassie about Sunny.

"Would you like to stay with me this morning, follow me around and get to know the other horses?"

Julie looked from her father to Cassie. "I'd like to stay with Cassie."

His eyebrows arched and she thought Loren gave him a kick under the table, but she wasn't sure. Maybe being too protective of his daughter was hurting her rather than helping her.

"Okay," Ben agreed. "I'll ride out with Uncle Loren for a little while, then I'll be back. I promise."

Cassie had the feeling Ben always kept his promises.

Fifteen minutes later, Julie trailed along with her dad and watched him saddle up a horse. As he mounted, she looked up at him and asked, "Can I ride one soon?"

"Maybe this evening when all the chores are done. Okay?"

She nodded. Then he stared at Cassie. "You'll keep watch over her?"

"I will," she agreed, meaning it. He still looked

torn by the idea of leaving. But then he and Loren rode out of the corral.

Julie suddenly looked as if she wanted to run after him.

Cassie crouched down beside her. "He will be back, you know."

"He won't fall off, will he?"

Cassie suppressed a smile. "No, he won't fall off. Loren taught him how to ride when he was a boy and that's something you don't forget." She could tell from the way Ben sat in the saddle, the way he used his reins, that he was a natural.

Rising to her feet she held out her hand to Julie. "Come on, let's go see Sunny. You'll have to stand at the gate while I go inside. Okay?"

Julie nodded that she understood.

Cassie took what looked like a cookie from her back pocket.

"What's that?" Julie asked.

"It's a special horse treat."

"Like a dog biscuit?" Julie asked.

Cassie laughed. "Exactly like that." Instead of opening the gate, she climbed over it and gently landed on her feet with a soft thud. Sunny looked away, her tail swished back and forth.

"Look what I have for you," Cassie said in a low voice. "Do you think you can come close enough to get it?"

The horse spied her and seemed to sniff the air. Then she took a few steps closer and Cassie stood perfectly still. "It's good," Cassie told her. "It's even good for you."

She stretched her hand out a little farther. Sunny was slow to move, wary of each step. She pawed the ground, eyed Cassie, then came close enough almost to touch. Cassie didn't breathe.

The horse quickly snatched the cookie from her hand, chomped it, then turned and loped toward the other side of the corral.

"Good girl," Cassie told her. "Thank you for trusting me." Then, knowing not to overstay her welcome, she climbed over the fence again and dropped down beside Julie.

"Why is she so scared of everyone?" Julie asked.

"She grew up in the wild, out in the brush and the trees with only other horses. Humans probably look to her like little green men would look to us."

Julie laughed. "But we don't have a spaceship."

"No, but we have cars and trucks. And all of those things scare her. She has to learn that it's good to be here, that I'm going to love her and ride her and take care of her."

Julie seemed to think about that.

"You were scared last night, weren't you?" Cassie asked.

"I wasn't when I went to bed because I knew Daddy was next door and you were in the other room. But then I had a dream and got really scared."

"Do you want to tell me about the dream?"

Julie shrugged, looked uncertain, but then said, "It was stupid."

"Not so stupid if it made you feel bad. Why were you scared?"

"Because there was thunder and lightning and wind, and I was all alone and I couldn't find Daddy anywhere."

"That is really scary. No wonder you woke up."

"But Daddy will always find me," Julie said, as if she were trying to convince herself of it. "He told me even if I ever get lost, he'll find me."

It was obvious that Julie was looking for a sense of security that her mother's abandonment had destroyed. "If your dad says that he'll always find you, then he will."

When Julie didn't seem to have anything else to say, Cassie knew better than to push it, so she suggested, "Come on. Let's go meet the other horses. You can touch Buttercup's velvet nose."

A smile broke out over Julie's face and she looked like the happy little nine-year-old that she was supposed to be. Taking her hand, Cassie led her into the barn.

Ben couldn't believe how good it felt to be back in the saddle again. He and Melinda had gone riding a few times when they were engaged, but that had been a long time ago.

When he dismounted in the corral, Clem, one of the younger hands, took the reins. "I'll groom her," he said.

"I walked her the last quarter mile so she's cooled down," Ben told him and Clem nodded.

"Is Miss Sullivan around?"

"In the barn with your daughter," Clem said, pointing.

Ben wondered how they'd spent the last hour. When he found the two of them he had to grin. They were mucking out a stall.

"Had about enough of that?" he asked Julie.

She shook her head. "I like working with Cassie. She fed Sunny a cookie. And you should feel Buttercup's nose. It's soft."

This was more animation than he'd seen in Julie in a long while and he had Cassie to thank for that.

"Can I go see what Sunny's doing?" Julie asked.

Cassie glanced at Ben but then told his daughter, "You can go watch her, but don't go near the gate."

"I won't," Julie said, and ran off through the barn and out the other door.

"Wow," he said. "What did you do to her?"

"Nothing. Why?"

"She's actually enjoying herself. At home I can barely get her to smile."

"Maybe that's because here she doesn't have things around her here that remind her what happened."

Ben had never thought of that. They were living in the house where they had been a family, where he'd thought they'd once been happy, where Julie had felt secure with two parents. Now, when she looked around at everything, she probably realized even more what she'd lost.

"How do you know these things?" he asked.

Cassie laughed, her brown eyes expressive and warm. "I know them because I was once a child who'd lost a lot. It's not so hard to figure out when you've gone through it."

He studied Cassie again, realizing how much he'd like to take her in his arms and kiss her. He had to admit, when he wasn't worried about Julie, he was thinking about Cassie and how she'd looked in her robe last night.

As if her thoughts had drifted to a similar vein, she asked, "Did Julie tell you what her dream was about last night?"

"No, she didn't. I asked but she was still crying and just shook her head. Why?"

"She told me she was trapped in a thunderstorm with wind and lightning and rain, and she couldn't find you and you couldn't find her."

"So she confided in you."

"I don't know if she confided. She just told me what it was about. I tried to reassure her that you'd always find her."

"Thank you," he said and meant it, suddenly feeling closer to Cassidy Sullivan than he wanted to feel. Something about the hushed atmosphere of the barn, the sunlight playing in the shadows, the way his daughter had confided in Cassie, seemed to make impulse more substantial than cold reasoning. He knew he'd just met this woman, though Loren often spoke of her with admiration for how she handled the ranch. Right now Cassie was as real as a woman could get and he was a man filled with sudden hunger that unnerved him as much as it urged him on.

There was a stray piece of straw in her hair, and he couldn't help but reaching out and lifting it away. Her hair was the color of aged whiskey, beautifully dark brown with a few red highlights. That was probably from the sun. As his fingers slid through the strands of her hair, she looked up at him. He was bowled over by desire that was as foreign as being back in the saddle again was. Before he considered the consequences, he slid his hand under her hair, tipping her chin up to him.

The next few moments changed everything.

She didn't move away...in fact, she leaned a little closer. The underlying message was clear—she was attracted to him, too. His lips met hers and passion became a part of his life again. He slid his tongue into her mouth and she responded tentatively at first, then with more confidence. Her hands gripped his shoulders and they were locked together in need, and hunger and a desire for more.

But then Cassie suddenly broke away.

He took in a huge breath, willed his raging hormones to desist, and shook his head in exasperation. "I never should have done that."

"I never should have let you. I don't—"

She stopped and he wondered what she was going to say. "You don't what?"

Cassie looked embarrassed. "I don't have affairs. I don't sleep around."

"I don't, either," he said simply.

When she studied him, he shrugged. "The last thing on my mind has been dating. Look, you're a very pretty woman and I've been living in the world of kids, carpooling and running my business. For just that one moment, maybe we both got transported."

She nodded. "I guess so." She seemed to compose herself and her embarrassment was gone. "I have to get back to chores. What are you and Julie going to do?"

"I'll take her for a walk down to the stream. We might spot some deer."

"Rachel made salads and there's roast beef left over for sandwiches. Go ahead and eat lunch whenever you'd like. I have to meet the insurance adjustor down at the guest cabin in a little while."

He knew the chores on the ranch kept Cassie busy. But he wondered if she was skipping lunch to avoid him, to avoid thinking about that kiss that was still singing in his blood, still arousing him. But he didn't put his question on the table because he didn't think he wanted to know the answer. He didn't like the idea of Cassie avoiding him. He didn't like it at all.

Chapter Four

That afternoon Cassie and Loren sat in her office. He was entering information into the computer on the massive wooden desk, telling her exactly what he was doing. She'd keep the expense numbers in her head.

He'd finished with last month's receipts when he leaned back in his chair. "Last month is looking good. Feed is down a little. Going into summer we won't be spending as much on utilities."

She nodded. Although she'd been listening, she was distracted by the call she'd received from Lucy this morning. "We're going to have more guests in two weeks."

"Lucy and Zack?"

"Lucy and Zack and...Gillian Bradley."

Loren's gaze snapped to hers. "The woman who found you for Lucy?"

"Yep. Lucy and I have decided we'd like to try to find our dad."

Loren narrowed his eyes. "What? I'm not good enough?"

Cassie laughed. "You're great and you know it. I don't know what I'd do without you."

"You'd have to tell everybody what's going on and they'd help you."

"It's just so humiliating needing help."

He gave her another look and she knew what that meant—that she should do something about it. She was just so scared. What if no one could teach her to read? She'd voiced that opinion to him before and he'd guffawed at it, so she didn't bring it up again now.

"Gillian and Jake are working a couple of cases so she can't get away until then. I thought Lucy and Zack could stay in the guest cabin. We should have it cleaned up and repaired by then. I'll give my room to Gillian and I can bunk on the sofa. It'll only be for a couple of days."

"Zack could sleep in the bunkhouse and you and Lucy could share the guest cabin," Loren offered with a sly smile.

"Give me a break. They're newlyweds. I'm not going to separate them."

"Separate who?" a deep male voice asked from the doorway.

When Cassie looked at Ben, she could remember the exact feel of his lips on hers, the excitement of having his arms around her. She sat up straighter in her captain's chair. "Lucy and Zack and a friend are coming in a couple of weeks. We were just figuring out the sleeping arrangements." She told him what they'd be.

"So I'll get to meet your twin."

"You'll do a double take," Loren advised him. "But there are differences."

Seeing what they were doing on the computer, Ben said, "I've got a great new program on my laptop. It's a lot easier than what you're using. It would take me about an hour to set it up for you."

"No, we don't want anything new." Though Cassie didn't actually use the program, she understood the columns and where everything was located. She could figure out the numbers if she had enough time. But something new would throw her off completely.

Loren's quick look at Cassie calmed her down as he told his nephew, "Let me think about it. There are advantages to changing and advantages to staying the same."

"You need to keep up with technology," Ben told him. "A ranch this size, with three hands on your payroll, it's essential."

"Like Loren said, we'll think about it." Cassie's cell phone buzzed and she slipped it out of her pocket. She didn't bother to check the ID but held it to her ear.

"Miss Cassie, Sunny got out of her corral! She's headed for the north pasture."

Cassie didn't wait to hear more. She shoved her phone into her pocket and ran outside. Cassie ran beyond Julie, who was sitting under the large cottonwood playing with her dolls.

Ben was right behind her. "Where are you going?"

"Sunny got out somehow. She's not used to fences and there's barbed wire all over Twin Pines."

"I'll ask Rachel to watch Julie and I'll come with you."

Clem had already led Cassie's horse into the corral. Ben went inside for another. Cassie climbed on her favorite grey named Whisper and rode toward the north pasture, without giving thought to anything but Sunny and the harm she could do herself. When she heard the clomp of a horse's hooves beside her, she glanced over her shoulder and saw Ben galloping toward her on a bay with a black mane named Dixie.

They raced at breakneck speed, the wind whipping Cassie's hair behind her until they spotted Sunny nibbling grass around some cedars. But as soon as she got a whiff of them she took off, heading toward a barbed wire fence. Scared out of her wits for her, Cassie tried to head her off. But just when she thought she had her turned, Sunny changed course again.

Attuned to Cassie's strategy, seeing where Sunny was headed next, Ben rode up on the inside to keep Sunny from going near the fence and turned her in the direction of the barn. They herded her, one on either side. Closer to the barn, they hung back, hoping she'd slow down. Sunny headed for a stand of pines, and then finally slowed.

Cassie said, "I'm going after her. I've got to clip a lead on her. I don't want her heading back toward that wire."

"Cassie—"

"It's okay, Ben. I know what I'm doing."

The look on his face said he didn't believe her.

Slowly, Cassie dismounted, then with a lead rope in her hand she approached Sunny a step at a time. She remembered when Sunny had taken the cookie from her hand and she hoped the horse was remembering, too. Reaching into her back pocket she realized a piece of that cookie had broken off. She grabbed it and took another step.

Sunny whinnied and pawed at the ground, but she didn't run off, and Cassie saw that as hopeful. All she had to do was distract the horse while she clipped on the lead. All she had to do.

Sunny's ears twitched and she blew breath from her nostrils. But she seemed interested in what Cassie had in her hand.

Cassie murmured to her as she approached. "Remember this? You really don't want to be out here all by yourself where you can run into things that will hurt you. Right?"

The brush swished around Cassie's boots and the breeze flapped her shirt. She kept her attention focused on Sunny and took that last step. As Sunny nuzzled the cookie from her hand, Cassie clicked the lead onto the halter. But the click must have scared her. Sunny reared up and took off with Cassie hanging onto the rope! Still holding on, her feet flew out from under her.

Moments later Ben rode up beside Sunny and grabbed the rope. "Let go!" he told Cassie.

As she did, he was the one with the lead in his hand and she could see he wasn't about to let go. But if he got pulled from his horse—

She quickly mounted up and galloped to the other side of Sunny, herding her closer to Ben.

Wedged between the two of them, Sunny slowed, snorted, then came to a halt.

"Thank you," she said completely breathless now, her hand and arm hurting from the fall and the abrasions.

"I didn't do anything but hang onto her like you did."

But he had done something. He'd protected her from further harm, protected Sunny, and showed that he cared as much about animals as she did.

Slowly, they walked Sunny back to the barn. Once there, Cassie slid from her mount and let Ben open the corral's gate. Then she led Sunny into her own corral, unsnapped the lead and let her go. When she closed the gate, she checked the latch. Had Sunny somehow nosed under it?

Ben waved to Julie and shouted, "Are you okay?"

Rachel was sitting with her under the tree, dressing one of her dolls.

Rachel waved back. "We're good. Barbie's going to a party."

Cassie heard Ben laugh and liked the sound of it. He hadn't done that since he'd arrived, and he needed a lightness of spirit as much as Julie did. He took their horses into the barn, unsaddled them and began to groom Dixie.

Cassie brought another grooming brush from the tack room, then went to Whisper. "I don't know how she got out," Cassie said with some frustration. "I can't let that happen again. Maybe I'll have to put a different kind of latch on the gate. It's old and it could have slipped."

They groomed the horses in silence, but it was a warm inviting silence. They'd done something important together and they felt it.

After they led their horses into the stalls, Ben asked her, "Are you all right? You took quite a tumble."

"I'm fine."

With an arched brow and an I-don't-believe-you look, he took her hand and turned it over, palm up. The rope abrasions were red and nasty. Then he scoped her arm and ran his thumb along the edge of a nasty scrape.

She no longer felt the scrape. She just felt his touch, the warmth of his skin and his tenderness.

"I couldn't forget about our kiss," he admitted, his voice husky.

"I know what you mean."

He gently slid his hand under her chin, smoothed his thumb over some dust on her cheek, and bent his head. The next thing she knew, his arms were around her and she was melting against him, full body press to full body press. Something about Ben was like a powerful magnet and she got swept up into desire and womanly needs she didn't even know she had. When she slid her fingers into his black hair, when she kissed him back as if she wanted passion as much as he did, she didn't think about where they were or who he was or who she was. The scent of leather and hay and Ben was all she took in. Her breasts pressed against his chest and his hand sliding down her back seemed so right.

"I don't know what I'm doing," he said, breaking away, ending everything they'd just been to each other in a few words. "I'm not ready for this and Julie—" He shook his head. "She certainly isn't ready for any more changes."

Cassie looked up at him wanting to say, But you need a new life and so does Julie. But she didn't say it because she knew she wasn't the one to provide it. She wasn't the type he needed or would want in the future. Sure, she might satisfy a physical desire now. But what happened when he returned to Vermont? And what happened when she stayed here? Heartache, that's what would happen.

Cassie wrapped pride around herself and stood straighter. "Getting run ragged by Sunny made us a little crazy."

"Crazy," he agreed, though he didn't sound as if he meant it.

"Speaking of Julie," Cassie said, getting back on the right footing, "Rachel has a granddaughter. I thought maybe she could bring her along tomorrow. She's Julie's age and I think they'll get along. Sue Ann is a great kid. Do you think that would be a good idea?"

"I think that's a great idea. Thanks for thinking of it." He motioned to her hand and arm. "Do you need help with those abrasions?"

"No, I'll go up to the house and clean off. I have some salve Loren swears by."

"While you're doing that, I'll load that computer program onto your computer. You can look at it and see if you like it. If not, I can always delete it."

A computer program. Instructions she couldn't read. She'd deal with all that later. Right now she had to deal with brush burns and cuts, and a kiss that had shaken up her world once again.

When Ben lifted Julie onto Buttercup, a nice-sized quarter horse perfect for her. Cassie was struck anew at the loss she felt at having never known a father. Ben adjusted Julie's hard hat so it sat just right, then showed her how to hold the reins. He was patient with her, keeping his arm around her until she felt secure. Then Julie smiled up at him and shook her head, ready to go.

Cassie stood to one side as Ben led Julie's horse in a huge circle around the corral. She giggled every once in awhile and Cassie had to smile. There was nothing like the feeling of being atop a horse. If Julie became attuned to riding easily, if she learned balance quickly and self confidence that she could guide the animal, the corral would soon become too small and she'd want to venture out. Cassie had seen that happen with other kids. Now and then she gave a few lessons. Nothing could teach a child self confidence quicker than learning to ride a horse. Or a teenager, she thought, remembering how she'd felt when she'd come to Twin Pines, not knowing if Tina would want her to stay longer than a few days, feeling as if nothing was permanent and nothing would last. Nothing did last. But she had more of a sense of permanence here than she'd ever had anywhere.

Suddenly Julie said, "Can Cassie lead me around for a while?"

Ben looked over at her to see if she was willing.

"Sure I'll lead you. Maybe we can even do a figure eight."

"What's a figure eight?" Julie asked.

Cassie took the lead rope. "I'll show you." Cassie guided Julie in a large figure eight and then a smaller one, so she'd have to lean right and then left to keep her balance. They were walking very slowly so it was easy to do.

"This is fun," Julie said. "Can we go a little faster?"

"A little faster." She walked at a brisker pace and Julie seemed at home in the saddle with it.

The sun was beginning to set as Ben came over to them. "I think we'd better quit for tonight, Cowpoke." He knocked his knuckle lightly on her helmet. "Time to get ready for bed."

Julie's face fell and she looked so disappointed. Ben must have noticed it because he assured her, "Every day we'll come out and ride a little more. Pretty soon you'll be holding those reins all on your own."

"You mean you'll let me?" Julie asked, her eyes brightening.

"In the corral. We'll see how that goes before we go outside of it."

After Ben lifted her off the horse, Julie surprised Cassie by running to her and giving her a huge hug. "Thank you for letting me use your horse. I like Buttercup."

Her throat tightening, Cassie bent to the little girl. "You are most welcome. And I think Buttercup likes you, too. You'll make a good team."

When Cassie's gaze met Ben's she saw respect for her there. She'd worked all her life to earn respect from others. Seeing it in Ben's expression made her feel almost giddy. How crazy was that!

But then she wondered how far his respect would go when he found out she'd almost landed in juvenile hall, when he found out she'd never finished high school, when he found out she couldn't even read one of Julie's storybooks.

During the next two weeks Cassie and Ben often worked side by side, repairing fence posts, holding each other's gazes much too long, trying not to inadvertently touch. That was easier when he spent time on his computer or on the phone and she was outside. But put them together in the same room and they seemed to gravitate to each other. She liked talking to him. He was a great listener. And he knew how to focus his attention on her as she felt listened to.

Rachel began bringing Sue Ann along each day, so Julie had someone to play with. Now and then Cassie got drawn into their play, making fairy houses under the cottonwood tree with old bark and sticks, cotton balls and toothpicks. She didn't remember playing like that when she was a little girl and it was easy for her to pretend along with Julie and Sue Ann. Ben began to trust her and Rachel to look after Julie for longer periods while he worked or when he rode out with Loren, Clem or Dusty to help with the cattle or summer repairs. He kept in contact with Cassie with his cell phone, and every time Cassie heard his deep voice she felt an answering response inside of her. But she still tried to stay away from his physical proximity. That last kiss had practically shaken her out of her boots.

One afternoon he came in from the barn and found Cassie in her office. Every once in a while she pulled out a rough plan she'd drawn for what she'd like to do with Twin Pines someday.

He was in the doorway studying her before she was even aware he was there. But then she was. "Hi," she said nonchalantly. "What's up?"

"Is it okay if I use your fax machine? My VP is sending me a document to look over, a new contract with a supplier."

She motioned to the fax machine. "I don't mind. The number's right there on the side in case anybody needs it."

Ben crossed to the machine, took a look at the number and seemed to memorize it. Then he noticed the sketches on her desk. "What's this?"

Only Loren knew about this project and her dreams associated with it. She intended to tell Lucy when it was more in the reality stage than the dream stage. But for some reason she felt comfortable sharing it with Ben. "I want to help troubled teens. I know what it's like being a foster child and never fitting in. I'd like to build guest cabins and bring teens to the ranch who need a break from their regular lives, those who would benefit from some one-on-one attention."

"You want to give them a place to go to fix them up rather than to tear them down."

"Exactly."

"That's a very unselfish thing to do."

"Not really. It's selfish of me because it will add meaning to my life."

"What puts meaning in your life now?"

She felt more drawn to Ben than she'd ever felt toward any man. "You've seen what gives my life meaning.

Running this place in a way that would make Tina Christopher proud. Giving back to the community when we can. Helping our neighbors. But sometimes living on the ranch is very isolating. It's easy to get self-concerned and I always want to be aware of the bigger picture. Do you know what I mean?"

"Oh, yes, I know what you mean. I had tunnel vision when Melinda and I were married, and maybe that's one of the reasons my marriage broke up. I couldn't see outside of that tunnel. I couldn't see that she and I needed more than passing each other like ships in the night. We needed more interaction with Julie so she knew how much we loved her. Families do often take love for granted."

"I try not to take anything good for granted," Cassie admitted."

Ben leaned down over her shoulder again to study the plans. "Do you want to build more cabins where the guest cabin is now?"

He was so close that she could feel his body heat. He was close enough for her to feel his strength. Her palms became damp and she realized her physical reaction to him was something she couldn't control. That really scared her.

"I'd like to put a row of them there, maybe five. Each cabin could sleep four."

"You'd have to hire on extra help."

"Tina left me an inheritance in a trust fund. What I'd like to do is start a foundation with it, maybe even get the community involved."

"If anyone can do it, you can. You're good with

people, Cassie—all ages. In fact, I wouldn't mind having you in my PR department."

She laughed, making light of his statement. "You might be glad I'm not in your PR department. Sometimes I'm a little too blunt."

"Sometimes honesty is better than a spin."

She felt as if she was being dishonest with him by not telling him she couldn't read. Sometimes she felt as if she were being dishonest with everyone. She'd learned tricks and strategies that made people think she could.

When Ben glanced away from the plans and looked straight at her, she was tempted to blurt out everything. But what good would that do? After all, he would be leaving. Still, that look in his eyes told her he wanted to kiss her again, maybe even do more than kiss her. And to her dismay she found herself vulnerable to that thought, even tempted by it.

Straightening and towering over her once more, he said, "I thought I'd warn you. Julie has something to ask you."

She waited.

"She'd like to know if you could help put her to bed tonight. She said she likes your stories about the horses roaming the range and maybe you'd tell her one before she falls asleep."

Whenever she spent time with Julie, they talked about horses. Cassie told her legends she'd heard and stories she'd picked up over the years. She'd explained she'd been to the Big Horns herself, watched the wild mustangs graze, seen them standing proud and tall on top of a hill. She'd even shown her some of the photographs she'd snapped. She hadn't been back to the Big Horns in a while. That would be a wonderful place to take Julie.

The idea that the nine-year-old wanted her to put her to bed meant one thing. She was getting attached. And Cassie was getting attached to her. Her worry must have shown in her eyes.

Ben said, "If you don't want to, that's okay. I'll head her off and tell her you're too tired."

"I like Julie and she likes me. When she follows me around the barn, we talk. When she watches me handle Sunny, we talk, too. But I don't want to do anything to hurt her, Ben. Is being around me going to do that when you leave?"

"I don't know. But I do know that you're good for my daughter and she needs you in her life right now. When we leave, maybe you can stay in touch."

She could stay in touch by phone. She couldn't stay in touch by e-mail. She was getting in deeper with Ben and Julie and she didn't know what to do about it. Maybe when Lucy arrived in a few days she'd have some advice. Cassie sure needed it from someone.

Chapter Five

Cassie had to tell Ben about Gillian. She'd be picking her up in less than an hour and the time had come to tell him the whole story. But would he think she was crazy?

No matter, really. He'd see how Gillian worked when she was here so he might as well know what she and Lucy were up to.

The barn was still except for the sound of a fork spreading hay. Ben was in Whisper's stall. As she approached him, butterflies fluttered in her stomach. Whenever their gazes met or they accidentally touched, the sizzle that was in their kiss tingled through her all over again. But she had something other than Ben's kisses on her mind today.

He looked up and tipped his hat, one he'd bought on his trip into town with Loren last week. He'd bought Julie a smaller version.

"Do you have a minute?" she asked him.

"I don't think Whisper's going to mind a slight delay in getting his bedding changed."

When she smiled, Ben set aside the pitch fork. "What's going on? Did Julie ask you to take her on a trail ride again? She told me she wants to ride as far as the stream."

"She's riding like a pro."

"That's because she has a good teacher."

Compliments flustered Cassie, especially right now. She wanted to step closer to Ben yet she knew she shouldn't. Everything about him was so...male. The top two snaps on his shirt collar were open and he'd rolled up his sleeves to his elbows. He was getting tanned from his work in the sun. And he looked...like any sexy cowboy should.

Veering away from that train of thought, she said, "I need to tell you something about the guests who are coming."

"Your sister and brother-in-law?"

"Well, actually the guest who's coming with them, Gillian Bradley. She's flying in from California for a reason."

His brow furrowed under his hat brim. "I don't understand."

"Remember, I told you Lucy found me last November?"

"Yes, of course."

She took a moment to think about what she was going to say, then plunged ahead. "She didn't find me by conventional means. The two of us left the hospital as Baby Sullivan #1 and Baby Sullivan #2. My mom put Lucy up for adoption but she kept me."

Ben didn't say anything, just listened.

"A lawyer handled Lucy's adoption as a private transaction with the McIntyre's lawyer, a Mr. Buckley. Last year Mr. Buckley contacted Lucy to tell her the other lawyer had died and he'd received something she might be interested in. It was a baby picture of the two of us in the hospital. All she knew was our mother's name, and all she had was that picture. No one had known she had a sister."

"But you said your mother was killed when you were five."

"Yes. So Mr. Buckley couldn't find any more than that. He had no idea what my name was."

"So it could have been Sullivan, or you could have married or you could have moved out of state."

"Exactly."

"So how did Lucy find you?"

This was the sticky part and there was no way to soft-peddle it. "Zack had hired on at Lucy's parents ranch at the time. He knew of this team in California. One person, Jake Donovan, was a reputable private investigator. His partner, Gillian, had a specialty of finding missing persons and a 99% success rate."

Ben's eyebrow arched. "That's pretty good. This is the Gillian you're talking about?"

"Yes. But Gillian isn't a private investigator. Gillian is—" Cassie took a deep breath. "Gillian can sense things from bonds a person has with someone else. She came to see Lucy, and through the picture and Lucy, she…saw my first name. She saw the arch at the entrance to the ranch and the Twin Pines there. So with that information her partner used his skills and they found me."

"Wait a minute. You said Gillian senses things. Are you telling me she's a psychic?"

There was something about that word that was so off-putting to people, maybe because people who pretended to be psychics and weren't were just charlatans. But she knew Gillian was the real thing.

"Yes, I am."

He frowned. "And why are you telling me this?"

"Because Lucy and I want to find our dad and that's why Gillian's coming here. The one thing that I've kept all these years that belonged to my mom was a pocket watch. It was special to her in some way and I don't know how. Maybe it belonged to her dad. I don't know. But Gillian is flying here so we can explore the possibilities."

"That's an expensive possibility," he muttered. "You could have mailed it."

"She told me not to. She didn't want it passed through lots of hands and she didn't want it to get lost. She said it's important to maintain its integrity. And as far as it being expensive— She and Jake started a not-for-profit foundation. If someone can't afford the daily expenses or their flight travel, they take it out of the funds that come in. Clients who do have money donate. Word is out about what they do and they have other donations rolling in, so this doesn't have anything to do with money."

He looked as if he wanted to say something but was holding back.

"What?" she prompted.

"I just find this hard to believe. Loren knows about it?"

"Yes. And Rachel." Ben was studying her so hard she thought he was trying to see everything she was and maybe everything she might have been. That scared her.

Finally he said, "You are one complicated cowgirl."

She wasn't sure whether or not that was a compliment. "Is that good or bad?"

"I don't think it's either, it just is." He came a little closer to her, looked as if he wanted to touch her, yet he didn't. "I suppose you want me to put all my preconceived notions aside and keep an open mind?"

"Something like that. After all, when Julie told me you knew how to braid her hair and tie little bows on the end, I didn't even blink."

A laugh burst from him and she smiled back, feeling closer to him than she wanted to feel.

"All right," he agreed. "I'll promise to keep an open mind if you'll do me a favor."

"What?" she asked warily.

"Sit down with me and let me explain the new computer program that could make bookwork easier. Loren isn't willing to switch over until I have your okay."

Could she get through that without Ben finding out her secret? Sure, she could. She was quick on her feet. She could listen and remember. It wasn't as if she'd have to actually read anything on the computer. All she had to do was listen.

"Okay," she agreed. "One day when I have some time." After all, she could postpone the lesson.

She was ready to step away, but Ben laid a hand on her arm. "You realize, I haven't sought you out lately because I didn't think you wanted me to. Julie's a buffer when she's around, but when it's just the two of us we could probably get into major trouble."

"Yes, we could." She had to be honest with him. "Ben, I don't know what I want. You make me feel something I've never felt before. But I don't want to be a temporary fix for you. I don't want to be a vacation escape."

She saw something flicker in his eyes. Respect? Admiration for her honesty? Yet she knew she could tell him about her inability to read and in an instant that respect would disappear. "I have to change and drive to the airport."

When she started to go, he caught her arm. "I will keep an open mind."

She could only hope that that was true.

When Cassie picked up Gillian at the airport, Gillian said, "You and Lucy are almost identical!"

"Almost?" Cassie knew most people who saw her and Lucy together thought that they were.

"Your hair's darker and Lucy has this dimple that appears when she smiles."

"My goodness, you do pay attention to detail."

"I'm not sure it's always a blessing," Gillian said with a laugh.

Gillian Bradley had light brown hair, and pretty brown eyes. She was a few years older than Cassie, but right away Cassie got a good vibe off of her. "Lucy tells me you have a little boy."

"Yes, I do. Matthew. He's with his dad right now. I think Nathan was going to take him to SeaWorld so he didn't miss me too much."

"This must be hard on you and your family."

"Well, as Lucy probably told you, I brought Matthew along when I visited her. Sometimes I do that. And I really don't travel that much. A lot of my work is local. But it's for a good cause and as Matthew grows up I think he'll see that."

They began walking toward the exit. "Your husband understands?"

"Oh, yes. I helped Nathan find his ex-wife and daughters, so he personally knows how important this work is."

"I don't know if finding our dad is as important as finding a missing child."

"Finding a loved one is always important," Gillian said without hesitation.

And so it went.

On the drive back to Twin Pines, they talked as friends would and Cassie felt relieved about this whole adventure.

As they drove under the arch with its wooden sign proclaiming Twin Pines Ranch, Gillian smiled. "That's exactly what I saw. I'm still amazed sometimes."

"Do you get clear pictures?"

"They're more sensations than they are like video clips or photographs. But sometimes a picture seems as clear as a Google satellite search."

At the ranch, Zack and Lucy came to meet them. They gave hugs all around. Loren said, "I already introduced your sister and her husband to Ben and Julie."

Ben had stood back while the group said their hellos. But now Cassie brought Gillian to meet him. "Ben O'Donnell, Gillian Bradley. And this is Julie O'Donnell," Cassie said, not forgetting about his daughter.

Gillian shook Ben's hand, then crouched down to Julie. "It's good to meet you. I hear you're staying here for a few weeks. Are you learning to ride?"

At first hanging back shyly, Julie now studied Gillian. "I ride Buttercup. She likes carrots and apples."

"Maybe you can take me to meet Buttercup while I'm here."

Rachel had made a late lunch and they all went inside to sit around the large pedestal table. Conversation flowed easily, about the ranch, life in California, winters in Vermont. Rachel's chili and cornbread were a big hit, as was her chocolate cake with peanut butter icing.

After dessert, Julie asked if she could be excused to play with her electronic game and Ben told her she could. The others looked at Gillian expectantly.

She glanced from Lucy to Cassie. "Do you want to start?"

They both nodded.

Lucy's husband, Zack, spoke up. "So that means we need to clear the room. I know how this works. I've been through it before."

"You don't like anyone to watch you while you work?" Ben asked, sounding a bit suspicious.

"It's not like that," Cassie responded, already protective of Gillian.

"No, it's not," Zack quickly agreed. "When Gillian came to help Lucy, I was around. Lucy and I were...beginning to get involved. My presence in the room made it more difficult for Gillian to tune into Lucy, so the same would be true for all of us. None of us have a connection to the information they need, so we'd just get in the way."

Gillian explained to Ben, "Think of bonds between people as current that can get interrupted."

"So if Zack stayed in the room with Lucy—" He trailed off.

"That would be like an extra crackle I don't need," Gillian answered with a smile.

Ben's gaze went to Cassie and she knew exactly what he was thinking. They both looked at Gillian and she gave a little shrug and said simply, "Yep, lots of bonds in this room today."

Though no one else knew what she meant, the two of them did. Pushing away from the table, Ben said gruffly, "I'll keep Julie occupied."

"Maybe Lucy and Cassie and I can just find a quiet place where we can talk."

"Why don't we go up to my bedroom?" Cassie suggested. "That's going to be your room while you're here. You can make yourself at home."

After Rachel offered, "I'll clean up here. You go ahead," Cassie gave the housekeeper a hug. "Thank you."

Rachel gave her a tight hug back. "No thanks necessary. I told Miss Tina I'd watch over you and that's exactly what I'm doing. Go on now, get started. See what you can find out."

When Lucy and Gillian started up the stairs, Ben

stopped Cassie before she could follow them. "I want to wish you luck. I obviously have my doubts about this, but I can see you don't."

"Can't you see Gillian is genuine?"

"I can see a woman who seems very nice...and ordinary, too."

"She caught on to what was happening with us."

"I'm not sure anyone has to be a psychic to catch on to that."

He was probably right.

She couldn't keep her gaze from his for very long. She couldn't help looking at him and thinking about what might be. Maybe it was the same for him.

Proving that it was, he wrapped his arm around her middle and brought her close for a quick but thorough kiss.

When he stepped away, he said, "I just wanted you to take some good energy with you."

She couldn't help but laugh. "I'll come find you when we're finished and tell you what happened."

"I'd like that." Then he went into the living room, picked up his laptop and went to the sofa to sit beside his daughter.

Cassie ran upstairs, hoping she'd find out more about the past and a father she'd never known.

In her room, Gillian sat on the bed with her legs crossed and motioned for Lucy and Cassie to do the same. "I'd like to talk about some of your memories. Can you do that?"

With her chest tightened a bit, Cassie admitted, "I don't remember much. My life was unsettled going from one foster home to another. My past got mixed up in what my future was and what I didn't want it to be. Do you know what I mean?"

"Yes, I know what you mean. You were in a situation you didn't like and you couldn't get out of it. You tried to convince yourself before each change that bad memories didn't matter, yet you were afraid to hope for anything better. Right?"

"Yes, that's exactly it."

"But that doesn't mean you don't have some good memories tucked away in there. You told me you took two things with you the night you left the apartment where you and your mom lived."

"It was an apartment above a garage. Just one big room and a bathroom," Cassie explained.

"Okay. You took away a stuffed toy and the watch, right?"

"Yes."

"Do you still have that stuffed toy?"

Cassie exchanged a look with her sister. She thought Gillian would want the watch and start with that, but apparently that wasn't the way she worked. Cassie had carried it in her pocket this morning, not knowing exactly when Gillian would want to start or where. But now she climbed off the bed and went to her closet.

Up on the shelf on top of all her clothes, she reached into a safe corner and pulled down a horse. He was brown with black ears and mane and a red bow around his neck. The red bow was fairly new. She changed it every once in a while, maybe as a homage to the child she'd once been.

Carrying the horse to the bed, she plopped it in front of her. "There he is."

"What was his name?" Gillian asked.

"Choco. Because he was the color of chocolate."

"Do you remember how you got him?"

The horse's mane urged her to rifle her fingers through it. "One of Mom's boyfriends gave him to me."

"Did she bring many men home?" Lucy asked.

"No. Not that I can remember."

Cassie closed her eyes and tried to go back, which wasn't something she did very often. "What I remember most is that he was really tall and he had this belt buckle that was so big and shiny I couldn't stop looking at it. One night he came for supper and he had this horse with him. I don't have a real sense of time but I think that was about a year before Mom was killed."

Gillian nodded then asked, "Do you mind if I hold it?"

"No, go ahead."

She watched as Gillian held the horse, felt his fur, straightened his bow. "You and your mom didn't have much but you were happy."

"I believe we were. Sometimes the only food we had was the meal mom brought home from the restaurant. Once in a while, the woman who stayed with me while mom worked, brought me cookies she baked."

"Your mom didn't like taking handouts," Gillian said.

Surprised, Cassie said, "No. She didn't. She wouldn't take them for herself, but she would for me." Again, Cassie glanced at Lucy and she said something she'd told Lucy before. "Mom really had to love you to give you away. You know that, right?"

As if Lucy couldn't find her voice, she just nodded.

"Do you remember anything before Choco came along?"

"Not much. Alan said—" She stopped. "His name was Alan. I'd forgotten that."

"So before Alan, what do you remember? Think about the room where you lived, the color of the furniture, and any decorations on the wall."

Cassie closed her eyes. "Nothing on the walls. They were dark...really dark. Paneling maybe."

"Did you have a TV?"

"A little one with one of those aerials attached. We got one fuzzy station. I used to stay there and watch cartoons if Mom had to go out for something."

"Were you scared?" Gillian asked.

"Not when I was watching cartoons. If it went really long and they went off, or the TV got really snowy, I can remember hunching up on the sofa with a cover over my head. But Mom usually wasn't gone that long or Flo was with me."

"Flo?"

"The woman who lived in the house near the garage."

"So you learned how to be alone when you were very little."

"I guess I did. I know I'm looking back now, and not really remembering. But I had this feeling that my mom was lonely."

"What makes you think that?"

"The way she'd take out the watch and look at it.

This expression would come over her face, maybe happy, maybe near tears, maybe a combination of both."

"Do you have the watch?"

Suddenly reluctant, not knowing exactly what giving it to Gillian would lead to, Cassie hesitated. But then she slid the suede pouch out of her pocket and handed it to Gillian. "That's what she always kept it in."

Gillian closed her eyes. Then she set the timepiece on the bed in front of her and said to Lucy and Cassie, "Hold my hands. Okay? And each other's."

They did as she requested and she looked down at the watch. "Your mom's nickname was Jannie?"

Lucy looked to Cassie.

But Cassie shook her head. "My babysitter—the woman who lived in the house near the garage—always called her Jeannette. I don't remember anything else."

"Maybe only one person ever called her that," Gillian said. "Maybe only Walt called her that."

Cassie held her breath as she waited for more.

Chapter Six

Gillian let go of their hands and just stared at the watch. "His name was Walt and I know you want answers, but I don't have them. I am getting a strong feeling that we need to do something more than just sit here and look at the watch." She gave them a smile.

"What else can we do?" asked Lucy.

"That depends on Cassie. Cassie, what are you willing to do?" Gillian asked.

"I don't understand."

"I don't exactly, either," Gillian admitted. "But I wonder if the garage in Laramie where your apartment was is still standing."

It had been years since Cassie had even thought about that small apartment and Flo—the woman who'd looked after her and lived in the house. "I don't know. I haven't been back there since I drove out of town that night and ended up in Cheyenne."

"When did you last see the apartment? When you were five?"

"No. One day when I skipped school, I found the place again. I think I just wanted to try to remember my mother. "Lucy squeezed Cassie's hand and she felt her throat tighten unbearably.

"So you know the address?" Gillian asked gently, seeing the difficulty she had when she remembered.

"It was 767 Seventh Street."

Picking up the watch, Gillian fingered it. "Laramie's only an hour from here. Are you willing to drive back there with me to see what we can dig up? I can call Jake. He's usually quick with public records and can find out something about the address. We could go today and be there before dark."

Cassie looked at Lucy. "Are you willing? You and Zack have a long drive back tomorrow."

"Let's do it," her twin decided. "We need this, Cassie, you know we do. Maybe we won't find out anything, maybe we will. But at least we'll know we've done something."

Cassie gave Gillian a nod. "All right. Call Jake."

A half-hour later, Cassie found Julie in the barn, sitting on a bale of hay, one of the many friendly cats in her lap. She smiled up at Cassie. "Tiger likes me."

"Well, of course, she likes you. You're petting her and giving her love. Is your dad in the tack room?"

Julie nodded. "That stuff smells."

Cassie laughed and went to find Ben. He looked up from his work cleaning one of the saddles when she stepped inside the room.

"How's it going?" he asked and she realized not only Julie was smiling more, he was too. He certainly looked more relaxed than when he arrived, even though she caught him several hours a day working on his computer, or on the phone to his headquarters.

"I'm going on a road trip in a little while with Gillian and Lucy. Just to Laramie. We'll be back tonight."

Cocking his head, he studied her carefully. "So, Gillian figured out something?"

Cautiously, Cassie began, "We don't have much, but—"

"You told me to keep an open mind and that's what I'm doing. If you don't want to tell me that's fine, but if you do, that's fine, too."

There was something about Ben's strength that gave her pause, something about his honesty that reminded her very much of Loren. "I gave Gillian the pocket watch and she feels very strongly that it belonged to a man named Walt. I still don't know who that is, if it was someone who passed in and out of my mother's life, or if it was my grandfather. But I think she also sensed that he used to call my mom Jannie. Her name was Jeannette, and I never heard anyone call her that."

"A term of endearment."

"Possibly." Then, taking a deep breath, she confided in him about the rest—the stuffed horse and the way she'd hidden the watch.

"Cassie, I'm so sorry. For a five-year-old that had to have been terrible."

"I think I just stuffed everything I'd felt about all of it for a lot of years. That's probably why I don't have many memories of when my mom and I were together. So Gillian feels strongly that if we go back to that apartment where I once lived, I might remember something else. So we're going to drive there and see what we can dig up."

Crossing to her, Ben settled his hands on her shoulders and looked deeply into her eyes. "I hope something comes of this for you."

"If you're trying to warn me that I might come home not knowing any more than when I leave, I understand that. I'm used to disappointment. And no matter what, Lucy and I will still have each other."

"That's right."

Ben's gaze held hers for several long moments, and then he slid his hand under her hair and nudged her a little closer. His voice went low. "Julie's not too far away so I can't kiss you like I'd like to kiss you. But when you get back, maybe we can remedy that."

Her pounding heart reminded her of Sunny's hooves as the mustang galloped around the corral. It was so loud she could hardly hear herself think. It caused such a sense of anticipation in her she couldn't find any words.

"If you need to talk on the way, while you're there, afterward, you have my cell number. Sometimes it's hard to share what we're afraid of most with the people closest to us."

She raised her chin. "You think I'm afraid of something?"

He ran his knuckle over her cheek. "No, not you. You'd never be afraid of anything, right?"

It was so hard for her to let her guard down, so hard for her to trust, especially someone like Ben. He was trying to make it easier, but trusting was never easy. So she simply responded, "I have your number."

Flinging his arm around her shoulders, he hugged her close to him for a few seconds and she felt that strength that was so much a part of him. She also felt everything she didn't want to feel—excitement, desire, even expectation.

At least she'd have something else to think about on the ride other than what she and Lucy and Gillian might find in Laramie.

It was about an hour later when Ben finished in the tack room and went to find Julie who was playing with the cats outside.

"I wonder if Rachel's making hot dogs for supper?"

"Why hot dogs?" he asked, thinking about weekends in Vermont and how he cooked hot dogs for at least one of their meals because they were easy.

"Because I told her I like them and she said she'd make things I like."

"We can go ask her."

"I want to ask Cassie if I can bring Tiger up to my room. Let's go find her."

Maybe Julie hadn't been in the barn when Cassie left...or had been playing with the cats behind the stack of hay bales. "Honey, she's not here."

"Where is she?"

His daughter's expression worried him. It was that haunted look she'd had before they'd arrived. "She had to go to Laramie. That's what she came to the barn to tell me."

"She didn't tell me."

"I think she was in a bit of a hurry." He knew Cassie had had one goal—to reach Laramie and find out what she could about her childhood.

"I don't want Cassie to go away."

"She'll be back tonight. That's what she told me. She and her sister, Lucy, and that other lady that came to visit had to go away for a little while. But they'll be back."

"How do you know?"

"Because Cassie told me she would. Because Lucy's husband, Zack, is still here."

"That doesn't mean she'll be back! You and me were home, but Mommy still left. And she didn't come back."

Ben hadn't expected this reaction, not in a million years. Maybe he should have. He knew Julie and Cassie were getting attached—at least Julie was getting attached to Cassie. Was Cassie getting attached to his daughter?

He crouched down and put his arm around Julie. "Cassie said she'll be back, so she will be back."

"I don't believe you. You said you and Mommy would work things out, but you didn't. She left."

Although Julie tried to escape his hug, he held her tight. She began crying and he knew the tears were about everything that had happened over the past eighteen

months, not just what had happened today. At any other
time, he would call Cassie and let Julie talk to her. But
Cassie had enough on her mind right now. And Julie?
She'd have to learn that sometimes people did keep their
promises. Sometimes, people did come home.

"Which way now?" Gillian asked, relying on Cassie rather than the GPS.

From memory that hadn't gone as cold as she'd
thought, Cassie directed Gillian in the twists and the
turns, the lefts and the rights. It had been almost ten
years since she'd been here, but ten years didn't seem to
mean a lot to a town.

For her, everything had changed.

Oh, sure, there were some noticeable differences—
a convenience store here, new businesses there. But the
old-Western flavor was still the same, maybe done up
with a new coat of paint.

This had once been home, yet it hadn't been home.
Not after her mom died.

She could feel Lucy's gaze on her and knew she understood. From the back seat, Lucy had made few
comments, just let them all think about what was going
to happen next. At times during the ride Cassie had
thought of Ben, of all the things he didn't know about
her. But now, as they drove closer to her past, she
couldn't even think about her future.

After Cassie directed Gillian to the house, they
parked along the street. The end of daylight cast long

shadows and Cassie suddenly wondered what they were doing here.

"What are we going to do? Go to the apartment first and see if anyone is living there?"

"Yep," Lucy answered. "Come on. Let's see what we find."

"Something's telling me this is crazy," Cassie protested.

Gently, Gillian laid her hand on Cassie's arm. "But something's telling me this is the right thing to do."

With that, knowing that Gillian didn't do any searching lightly, Cassie wasn't going to give up after coming this far.

The house was a white clapboard bungalow. Behind it was a one-car garage that had a second floor and a stairway running up the side. They headed to the garage first.

Lucy gave Cassie a squeeze on the shoulder for encouragement, and then Cassie mounted the steps, needing to do this part alone. However, she knocked, and knocked again, and nobody answered. She couldn't peek in the door because a lacy curtain covered the glass.

Remembering all those years ago, she realized there'd been a lace curtain on it then, too. "I can't see anything," she said. "It's all dark. Let's go over to the house."

As they walked to the house's front path, Gillian said, "Jake told me a Florence Jean Shultz owns it."

Gillian hadn't given her this information before. "Flo," Cassie said, remembering more. Flo's hair had been red and she'd worn it in a topknot. She was the woman who had stayed with her when her mom worked. Flo had been with her the night her mother died. "I guess I shouldn't be surprised she still lives here. I'd just forgotten about her."

"Maybe it was just too painful to remember," Gillian offered, and Cassie knew she was right. Everything about that time had been painful.

She didn't know what to expect when she knocked on the door.

A light went on in the kitchen, and then there was the woman who absolutely looked twenty-one years older, but was still recognizable. Cassie felt as if she'd lost all her breath and she couldn't talk.

But Flo didn't recognize her. After all, a five-year-old and a twenty-six-year old looked very different. Cassie didn't consider herself a good judge of age, but Flo looked to be near seventy.

Cassie finally found her voice. "Mrs. Shultz? I'm Cassidy Sullivan. Do you remember me? It's been over twenty years, but—"

Flo put her hand over her mouth as if she couldn't believe Cassie was standing in front of her. "Oh, my goodness, Cassie! Is it really you?"

Tears filled Cassie's eyes and she put her arms around the older woman, giving her a gentle hug. "Yes, it's me."

"My goodness, dear, come inside. I have the fan going and it's not too warm. Would you like some cookies? I baked them for my grandchildren. Who do you have with you?"

At a loss because old memories swirled around her, Cassie didn't even know where to begin.

Fortunately, Lucy stepped forward. "I'm Lucy Burke. I found Cassie last year. I'm her twin sister."

"You do look alike. I have cataracts and can't see too well these days, but I can tell now. My goodness! That means Jeannette had another baby. I never knew that."

"Mom gave Lucy up when she was born," Cassie explained. "Gillian is the one who helped Lucy find me."

"Well, gracious. What a wonderful thing to happen. Come on, sit down."

They all settled around a small round table under the ceiling fan.

"I still can't believe you came back here after all these years," Flo said as she pulled a cookie jar to the front of the counter. What brings you here?"

"Well, actually," Cassie said, "I wanted to see the place where Mom and I lived. Are you renting it now?"

"I'm between renters right now. I posted a notice at the grocery store, but no one's called yet. Of course, you can see it. I haven't changed it much over the years. I never had the money for renovations. So it still has that old dark paneling and even the same tiled floor." She took a key from a hook under her cupboards. "I'll make some coffee and ice it while you go over and look around. You do have time for a visit, don't you?"

"Yes, we have time for a visit," Gillian assured her.

"The place is empty. I was going to try and clean it this week. So you'll see all the flaws."

"We're not looking for flaws," Lucy said, "just the memories."

Before they stepped outside the door, though, Cassie asked Flo, "How old was I when we moved in there?"

"You were only a few weeks old when your mom moved in with you. The pastor at our church told us about this young woman in a shelter who needed a place to live. The room over the garage was empty, so I offered. My husband Harry had been killed in a construction accident a few years before. My Tommy was in college then, and I was lonely here. I met your mother and we got along. I knew she had nothing to speak of and she needed work. Living here gave her a little time to get on her feet."

"She worked as a waitress, right? I remember her coming home with a uniform and an apron and sometimes she'd bring food."

"Yes, she was. She worked at a family diner a couple of blocks down. It's since closed up. While she worked I watched you. I had Harry's pension and I took in sewing."

"I remember you sitting on the sofa and working."

"Hemming skirts, most likely. I took in laundry to iron then, too, but I did that here. Go on, go take a look at where you lived and then we'll talk."

Five minutes later, they'd climbed the outside stairs and were standing on the landing at the apartment door. "It doesn't sound as if our father was around after we were born," Lucy said as Cassie unlocked the door. They went inside the small apartment.

It wasn't even an apartment, really, Cassie realized. It was one big room. There was a very small galley kitchen with a two-burner stove, a compact refrigerator and a bathroom off the living quarters.

All Cassie could do was stand there and study the dark paneling.

"Take a breath," Gillian said. "Don't think about everything you lost, think about what you had when you were here."

Turning around slowly, Cassie noticed there were shelves on brackets above the TV connection. Those shelves. Her mom had put things up there she didn't want Cassie to reach—the glass dish that usually held her keys, a tin box that held matches, dried flowers in a small pottery vase. And then Cassie remembered something else that had meant a lot to her mother. Her mom had gotten it down and looked at it often, almost as often as she'd taken out the watch. It had been a wood carving of a foal.

"Those shelves," Cassie murmured. "They held things mom didn't want me to get hold of. One of those things was a wood-carved foal." Her gaze met her twin's. "You carve. You showed me your workshop. You make horses, too. You gave me one for Christmas."

"Do you think our mom carved it?"

"I don't know. I never saw her do anything like that, not that I can remember. But what does a five-year-old remember?"

"That's something we can ask Flo about," Lucy suggested.

Weighed down by memories she didn't altogether understand, Cassie felt lost, deflated...as if they'd never have the answers they were searching for. "This is a wild goose chase, isn't it?"

Chapter Seven

With a concerned glance at Cassie, Gillian dropped to the floor and patted on it. "This isn't a wild goose chase. Your memories are getting stirred up and you're not comfortable with that. But they can help. Sit here and tell me more about the carving. I saw Lucy's work. It's beautiful."

With a sigh and uncertainty rolling in the pit of her stomach, Cassie dropped down onto the tile with Gillian and so did Lucy. Taking a deep breath, she closed her eyes. The foal Lucy had given her for Christmas sat in her room at the ranch on her nightstand. Every time she looked at it, she felt the love that Lucy had made it with. Now she wondered if there was more behind it.

"I'd forgotten all about that foal. I mean, whenever I looked at Lucy's horses it was like something would just be on the edges of my memory. Do you know what I mean?"

"Sure do," Gillian responded. "So pull in those edges. What are they about?"

"The foal that sat on that shelf was very much like Lucy's work. It had the same finesse, the same polish. My mom let me hold it once or twice, but she told me it wasn't a toy." Cassie suddenly looked at Lucy. "Are you upset Mom didn't even tell Flo about you?"

Lucy thought about it. "I could get upset at her for a lot of things, but I've chosen not to. If I were in her position, with no job, no place to stay, nobody to help me and I gave up my baby, I wouldn't want any reminders. I don't think I'd want to talk about it. She probably tried to put me out of her mind."

Recalling the years she'd spent in Laramie trying to forget rather than embrace the grief of losing her mother, Cassie admitted, "I should have tried to see Flo sooner. I guess I never thought she'd still be here. Time passes and life changes and you think everybody else's does, too."

Her gaze scoured the room, the ceiling with the stain from where water must have leaked in, the scarred planking low on the walls where a kid's shoes must have hit or rubbed or furniture scraped. The tile floor was cracked in places. But Cassie's memories were still limited to a few vivid pictures and she couldn't seem to reach beyond those to remember.

"I think we're done here," she finally murmured. "Let's go talk to Flo."

A half-hour later they were enjoying iced coffee and cookies and talking about when Cassie had lived in the apartment with her mom.

Flo filled in as much information as she could, but most of it was what Cassie already knew. "When they took you away that night," Flo said, looking disturbed, "I tried to convince myself they'd find a good family for you and you'd be happy."

"Foster families aren't always looking for a permanent child," Cassie told her, soft-pedaling what had happened. "A family moves away and the authorities have to find you another place. If you don't get along, they move you again. By the time I was a teenager, I was pretty rebellious and not many real parents can handle that. I just didn't fit anywhere."

Part of that problem had always been her fear that whomever she was staying with would find out she couldn't read. But no one had. Maybe they just hadn't cared enough to look and really see.

"As you said, the apartment is pretty much like it was when Mom and I stayed there. I noticed those shelves are still hanging on the wall. Can you tell me what happened to everything that was there once they took me away?"

Compassion filled Flo's eyes as she studied Cassie. "Not much belonged to your mom, honey. The furniture had been mine. I gave her clothes to Goodwill because I didn't know what else to do with them. I looked high and low for one thing that was valuable that your mom had. It was a gold pocket watch. But I couldn't find it anywhere."

With a trembling hand, Cassie pulled the pouch from her pocket. "You mean this? I took it with me. I pushed it into my stuffed horse so nobody would see it." She set the pouch on the table.

"Oh, I'm so glad you have it. May I?"

Cassie gave the watch a little push toward Flo.

Flo dumped the watch from the little pouch and opened it. "This was very special to your mom."

"Why?" Cassie asked, holding her breath.

"Because the man she loved gave it to her. He was your father."

When Cassie could hardly keep from jumping out of her chair, she saw Lucy's excitement, too. "Do you know his name?"

Flo's smile was sad. "No, I don't know his name. But one night when Jeannette got a little tipsy, she told me the love of her life had given her this. This and that little foal she kept on those shelves. He was an artist, she said, who couldn't make any money at it and he was traveling from place to place to find work and to do what he loved most—carving and painting."

With her heart beating so rapidly, Cassie couldn't speak.

Lucy jumped in. "We're here because we're trying to find him. Cassie has the watch and we didn't know who it belonged to."

Flo thought about it, as if she were dragging bits of old memories into place. "Your mom said his dad had given it to him."

"Do you know why he gave it to Jeannette?" Gillian asked.

"She never said, but I suspected it was because he had deep feelings for her. Maybe he didn't want to leave but he had no choice. He had to find someplace to make a living."

"I wonder why she didn't just go with him?" Cassie mused. "She didn't have anything tying her here, did she?"

"Not that I know of. But after he left, I don't think she ever heard from him again."

"So many questions," Cassie said, then thought of something. "So do you know what happened to that carving? The foal"

"Sure, I know what happened to it. I kept it! It's beautiful. It's in my bedroom. I'll go get it. It belonged to your mother and you should take it with you."

Cassie almost jumped out of her seat to follow Flo, but she didn't. She waited until the older woman returned, carrying the small foal in the palm of her hand. She handed it to Cassie as if she were passing on a sacred object.

When Cassie ran her thumb over the foal's head, over its little ears, over its body and its curled up hooves, shivers danced up and down her arms. It was truly beautiful, as beautiful as anything Lucy carved. She handed it to her twin.

Tears came to Lucy's eyes as she managed to say, "I must have gotten my talent from him."

The silence around the table was respectful and in memoriam of sorts, of their mom and their dad, who-ever he was.

Gillian asked, "Can I see it?"

Suddenly, anticipation filled Cassie. If this did belong to her father, like the watch, then maybe—

Gillian lightly passed her fingertips over the carving. Then she turned it over. Her thumb slid across the bottom of it and Cassie wondered what she was doing.

"Artists sign their work and your father did, too." She handed the foal to Cassie so she could see. She could barely make out the knife's strokes etched into the base and she handed it to Lucy. "Hunter. Is that what's carved there?"

"My guess is, Hunter was his last name," Gillian said, "and I'm still getting a strong sense that his first name was Walt."

"You think we have a name? Walt Hunter?" Lucy asked Gillian in breathless surprise.

"I don't know if you should get your hopes up, but Jake is very good with databases and dates." Gillian asked Flo, "So, Jeannette never mentioned Walter Hunter, or anything like that?"

Flo thought about it and shook her head. "She never mentioned his name. I had the feeling that thinking about him was very bittersweet for her. How did you know his name was Walt?"

To tell Flo, or to not tell Flo? But Cassie figured they didn't have anything to lose. So she explained exactly how Lucy had found her and how Gillian had sensed the name when she'd held the watch.

"Well, my goodness! I didn't think things like this actually happened for real, that it was only on TV and in the movies," Flo said.

"If we could get any other information it would be really helpful," Gillian told her. "My partner does all the computer work and the heavy analysis of data, so anything he can plug in would be great. Did you get any sense at all if Cassie and Lucy's father was the same age as Jeannette?"

Flo thought about it. "Jeannette was only nineteen, just out of high school. I got the impression that this man she loved was too young to think about responsibilities, too. Do you know what I mean? So I don't think he would have been much older."

"He could be anywhere in the world," Cassie concluded.

"That's true," Gillian agreed. "Or...he could be close by, too. People have patterns. They often return to places that hold memories for them, or they go back home. An age will help Jake target the name. He can start in Wyoming and branch out. Yes, it's looking for a needle in the proverbial haystack, and it could take time. But he rarely comes up empty-handed. If you'll excuse me, I'll give him a call, and then we should probably be starting back. I'll try to get a flight out tomorrow."

Cassie knew Gillian had a husband and son who were waiting for her to return home. She understood. She wanted to get back to the ranch and tell Ben what she'd found out.

Ben. Just what would he think about all this? Would he even care?

Almost eleven when they returned to the ranch house, Cassie, Lucy and Gillian found Loren playing Blackjack with Zack in the kitchen. After they'd said goodbye to Flo, Lucy had called Zack to tell him what had happened and then to add they were stopping to eat before coming home. None of them had wanted the men to worry.

Hardly in the door, Lucy rushed straight to her husband. Zack wrapped his arms around her and gave her a giant hug and kiss, a kiss that made Cassie think of her kisses with Ben.

She heard him murmur to her twin, "I'm glad your trip was successful, but I'm glad you're back, too."

"We don't know yet how successful," Gillian said. "It all depends on what Jake can find out. A couple of prayers wouldn't hurt."

"I do that every day," Loren assured her, "for all of you." He shot a look at Cassie. "If you're wondering where Ben is, he's upstairs sitting by Julie's bed. She had a lot of trouble getting to sleep tonight."

"Why? Did something happen?" She wanted to see Ben and tell him everything that had happened.

"You could say so," Loren said with a direct look. "She was pretty upset after you left."

Feeling sideswiped by that one, Cassie was puzzled and Loren obviously saw that. "Apparently you didn't tell her where you were going and you didn't say goodbye."

Remembering how she'd left the barn in a hurry, she hadn't spotted Julie anywhere in sight. But she hadn't looked, either. "What did she say?"

Loren shrugged. "Don't know for sure, but the gist is she thought maybe you weren't coming back."

"Oh, my gosh! I never even thought she'd associate my leaving with—"

"Her mother's?" Loren asked.

Feeling awful, Cassie wasn't sure what to do.

Zack nudged Lucy toward the door. "Come on, let's turn in. We have a long drive tomorrow. I talked to the builder today and I set up a meeting for next week."

Suspecting her sister and brother-in-law just wanted to talk about everything that had happened, and definitely wanted to spend time alone, she walked them to the door and gave both of them a hug, wishing them good-night. Turning to Gillian, she said, "I'm just going to grab my nightgown and robe from my room. Then you can turn in."

"I feel like I'm the one who should sleep on the couch," Gillian said.

"No way. You have a flight out tomorrow and you need your rest. I'll be fine. After all, I'm used to sleeping in the barn with the horses sometimes."

After Loren said his good-nights, Cassie followed Gillian upstairs, swiped her robe and nightgown from a hook inside the closet door, and then went to the door. But she stopped there and gave Gillian a hug. "Thank you so much. I don't know how I'm ever going to repay you."

"No repayment necessary. I love doing this kind of work for this very reason. But I have to warn you, Cassie, if we find this Walter Hunter, you can't let your expectations run away with you."

"You've seen situations like this that didn't go well?"

"I've seen situations go well and I've seen situations like this just sort of fade away. I know the saying's overused, but you really have to try to just go with the flow."

"I will. I promise. I'll see you in the morning."

Standing in the hall with her robe and nightgown slung over her arm, Cassie cast a glance at Ben's door. It was closed. But then she shot a look to Julie's door and it was ajar. Unable to help herself, she went over to the doorway and peeked inside.

Ben was sitting in the chair by Julie's bed, his legs propped up on the mattress.

When she pushed the door open a little farther, he dropped his feet to the floor and sat up straight. As he did, Julie asked, "Daddy, don't leave, okay?"

"I'm not going anywhere. But someone just came home and I think she wants to say good-night."

Cassie walked into the room, and Ben turned on the bedside lamp. But Julie didn't seem excited to see her. In fact, she looked even more upset.

Following instinct more than anything else, Cassie dropped her robe and gown on the side of the bed. "Hi, Julie," she said. "Is it okay if I come in and say good-night?"

Julie nodded but wouldn't look at her. That was strange.

Ben stood, apparently not knowing whether he should stay or go.

Cassie asked him, "Do you mind if I talk to Julie for a couple of minutes?"

"No problem. I'll just get a drink of water." He looked down at his daughter, worried. It was the same worried expression she'd seen the day he'd arrived. This was her fault and somehow she had to make it right.

After Ben left, she sat on the bed beside the nine-year-old. "Loren said you were upset when I left."

Julie nodded, still not looking at her.

"Honey, I'm sorry I left without saying goodbye. I

didn't see you when I was on my way out, but I should have made a point of finding you."

"I thought you weren't coming back." There was almost panic in Julie's voice.

"Twin Pines is my home. I'll always come back here."

"Mommy had a home, but she left and didn't come back. Daddy said I didn't do anything wrong. But here I did, and I was afraid you found out and that's why you left."

Julie was crying now and Cassie had no idea what she was talking about. She moved a little closer to her, put her arm around her shoulders and brought her close. "Hey! What could you have possibly done wrong? You've been making friends with Rachel and Loren and Sue Ann and all the animals."

Julie was silent a very long time. Cassie just waited, not wanting to push too hard. Something was weighing on Julie and she might as well get it off her chest, no matter how trivial or how big.

Finally, she blurted, "I let Sunny out. I thought she'd want to run and play someplace bigger. I thought it would be good for her. But then you were so upset and Daddy went and helped you. She could have gotten hurt." Julie was really crying now and Cassie just held her.

"It's okay, honey. She didn't get hurt and your dad and I didn't get hurt."

"You fell and got scraped."

"I did. But I've fallen and gotten scraped before." She leaned away from Julie now and looked deeply into her eyes. "Listen to me. I understand why you let her out. You didn't want her to feel trapped. You thought she'd be happier. She was used to being free and you wanted her to feel that way again. But here she has to learn a different life. Once she settles in, I'll let her run in the big pasture with all the other horses. She'll make friends and she'll play with them. And then I'll take her on long trail rides. She'll like that, too. But for now I'm doing what I think is best for her. Can you understand that?"

Julie sniffed and then slowly nodded. "Are you sure you're not mad? That's not why you went away today?"

"I should have explained to you why I went away. I'm not mad. I never even suspected you let Sunny out. But I'm glad you told me. It's always best to be honest."

As soon as the words came out of her mouth, she knew she should be following her own advice. Be honest with Ben, a little voice in her head told her. Yet fear kept her from doing that, just as it had kept Julie silent.

"You won't tell Daddy about it, will you?"

This was putting her in a sticky situation, but she felt her bond with Julie was becoming important, so important that trust needed to be built, not broken. So she said, "I won't tell your daddy about it, but I think you should."

Julie shook her head vigorously.

"He's not going to leave you. He loves you. He won't even be angry if you told him why you did it. I want you to think about it, okay? And if you want me with you when you tell him, I will be."

"I'll think about it," Julie said, and Cassie knew she would, because she was that kind of little girl.

Time passed as Cassie sat holding Julie, reassuring her not everyone in her life would leave her. She told her about looking for her own dad and hoping she could find him. She recalled funny antics from the different horses she'd owned and how they'd been her best friends. Finally, Julie snuggled down beside her and her eyes closed. Her breath became even and Cassie saw she entered a peaceful sleep.

At some point, Ben had come to stand in the doorway and he'd listened along with his daughter. When they both realized Julie was sleeping soundly, he motioned Cassie out into the hall. "Thank you. Whatever you said must have reassured her and calmed her down."

"I want to throttle her mother, I really do. How could she do this to her?" The outrage Cassie felt on Julie's behalf was palpable and she was sure Ben could feel it, too.

"Melinda is only concerned now with what she wants, not what Julie needs." He gave Cassie a slow smile. "Thank you for wanting to stand up for Julie. I think that's why she bonded with you from the beginning. She sensed that quality in you."

"Children need advocates. They need someone who will understand their deepest fears. That's the only way they can shake them off."

"And what's your deepest fear?"

That I'll tell you the truth about me and you'll turn away. But of course she couldn't say that. "I guess that I'll never find someone who feels as deeply about Twin Pines as I do, and who can accept me just as I am."

"Zack gave me and Loren a short version of what happened in Laramie. So now you have a name."

"Yes, we do, and I also have this." She had slipped the fawn into her blouse pocket over her heart. "I think Lucy and I are going to share custody of it because our dad made this. At least that's what we think." She held it out to Ben.

He took it, turning it first one way and then the other, admiring it. "Beautiful work."

"Lucy does similar work. She must have inherited the talent. The woman who let us stay in the room above her garage has had it all these years. I should have gone back there sooner, I really should have. I should have looked her up sooner. But even if I had, I don't think I would have figured it out. I mean, I never would have had his first name without Gillian's help."

"Amazing, isn't it?" he asked.

"Amazing." But they were gazing into each other's eyes and Cassie knew they weren't talking about Gillian's gift. No, they were talking about this connection they felt between the two of them.

Finally, Ben nodded toward Julie's door. "I'm going to sit by the bed a little while longer."

"And I'd better hit that couch. Five a.m. comes mighty early."

"I'll see you at breakfast."

"At breakfast," she repeated, suddenly wanting nothing more than to spend the night in Ben O'Donnell's arms.

Chapter Eight

Ben felt overwhelming pride in his daughter as he watched her guide Buttercup into the corral after Clem opened the gate. She was becoming a great little rider and wanted to go farther afield each time. Cassie was riding beside her, and he'd dropped behind. He watched as Cassie said something to his daughter and she laughed. He didn't know what had transpired between them last night in the bedroom before he'd walked in, but whatever it was, his daughter seemed to be on an even, happy keel again. Cassie certainly had the magic touch with her. He knew she was on pins and needles about what the private investigator was going to find out, if he was going to find out anything about her father. He'd seen the silent communication between her and Lucy before Lucy had left this morning. He'd seen the hug she'd given Gillian. They were all hoping for the best.

Since Julie had taken her first ride, Cassie had taught her how to help groom the horses. She was always right there with her to make sure she was safe. Ben realized he trusted Cassie more with Julie than he'd ever trusted his wife. Melinda had never seemed to really enjoy spending time with her daughter, to get down on her level and play with her and laugh with her and even talk with her. But Cassie had no problem doing that.

A half-hour later they were crossing the lane to the house to get lunch when the mail truck came rumbling down the gravel. After a minute or two, the driver jumped out with a large box in his hand with mail on top of it. Cassie took everything from the carrier, who looked to be about her age. Ben could see right away that they'd known each other for a while. They chatted a couple of minutes, then the carrier hopped back in his truck, pulled into the empty parking space at the barn making a U-turn, and headed back down the lane.

"I think it's the new harness I ordered," Cassie said. "It should be supple enough that Sunny won't mind it too much." Noticing Cassie didn't bother glancing at the address on the box, nor did she rifle through the mail once they'd gone inside, he nodded to the bills on top. "Pretty soon they won't come in the mail at all. I'm surprised you haven't signed up for email bill delivery."

A shadowed expression crossed Cassie's face that he didn't understand. It was there and gone so quickly he thought maybe he'd imagined it.

She answered simply, "Loren takes care of all that."

From upstairs Rachel called, "I'm changing the beds. I'll be down soon to start lunch."

"Take your time," Cassie called back.

Then she handed the pile of mail to Julie. "Can you take this back to my office and put it on the desk?"

"Sure can. Can I hang with you this afternoon? Dad wants to ride out with Loren."

When Cassie's gaze met Ben's, he shrugged. "I didn't say that."

"You know you want to, Daddy. And it's okay. Unless I'll be in the way," she said to Cassie.

"You won't be in the way. I'm going to work with Sunny for a bit, maybe try to put a blanket on her back. Maybe you'd like to try taking some pictures with my camera. Then you can show your dad how things go when he gets back."

"Yeah. Super." Julie hurried back the hallway with the mail.

"Are you sure you don't mind her being around?"

Cassie touched his arm and he felt fire shoot through his whole body. She looked up at him with such sincerity he wanted to...kiss her.

"You should know by now, Ben, I don't mind. You're lightening my load by helping Loren and I like spending time with Julie. Really." Her hand was still on his arm and he wanted to pull her close and feel her against him.

But just then, his cell phone buzzed.

Cassie backed away and he wished—he wished his life were simpler.

A short time later, as his manager and VP related production problems that had cropped up in the past twenty-four hours, Ben found himself pacing the living

room as he figured out what to do, told Greg what
documents to email him and gave him the best way to
approach the account that would be held up. "Tell Mr.
Salinger we'll give him a discount of 10%. If that
doesn't do it and he needs to talk to me, I'm available.
Don't hesitate to let me know if there are any more
problems."

After a few more instructions, Ben ended the call.

When he returned to the kitchen, Cassie was pulling salads from the refrigerator. She said, "Julie went
upstairs to 'help' Rachel."

He smiled. His daughter was involved here and he
liked that. She felt as if she was part of the household
and it didn't just revolve around her. "Great. Rachel
told her Sue Ann will be coming again tomorrow."

Cassie nodded to his phone. "Trouble?"

"Some. I'm hoping it'll all smooth out. I might
have to set up a video conference for later today."

"I'm impressed by the way you're handling your
company long-distance. That can't be easy."

"I have good people who work for me. That solves
a lot of problems right there. What I do isn't so different from what you do."

"How so?" When she tilted her head, her hair slid
over her shoulder and his fingers itched to stroke it.

Attempting to concentrate on their conversation,
he said, "I'm CEO of O'Donnell Carpet. You're CEO
of Twin Pines."

Again, he thought he saw a shadow pass over her
eyes. This time she didn't chase it away. She said, "It's
not the same at all."

He took her hands in his and held them. She seemed surprised but didn't pull away. "You downplay your strength. You downplay what you do in a day, from gentling a mustang, to overseeing how the hands handle the cattle, to keeping on the same wavelength with Loren and Rachel. Why do you do that?"

When she glanced away from him, he could sense she was ready to turn away, too. But he wouldn't let her. "Cassie," he said again, "why don't you believe in yourself?"

That made her spine straighten and her eyes flash. "I do believe in myself. I know I work hard. But I have a lot to live up to. Tina gave me all this."

"And you don't believe you deserve it? Is that the problem?"

Now she did pull away. "There is no problem, Ben. I don't know what you think you're seeing, but I'm capable. I work hard and at the end of the day I know I've done the best for Twin Pines that I can possibly do. That's what matters to me. But I'm not winning the Nobel Peace prize. I'm not finding a cure for cancer. I'm not running a company the size of yours. I know my strengths and I'm realistic about them."

This time they were interrupted by Loren coming through the door, who apparently could feel the tension in the air because he looked from one of them to the other. "Am I interrupting something?"

"No, of course not," Cassie answered, crossing to the refrigerator and pulling a pitcher of iced tea from it. "Are you going to join us for lunch?"

"No, I ate with the guys down at the bunkhouse. But I did want to tell you Fred Whittaker stopped by this morning while you were out riding." Loren explained to Ben, "When those storms went through, lightning struck his barn. It burned to the ground. Thank goodness the horses were in the pasture."

"So he's ready for a barn raising?" Cassie asked.

"Yep, he is. Everything's ordered for Saturday. He said Marilyn's starting to cook up a storm already. Are you going to be able to get away?"

"Of course, I'll come help."

Loren glanced at Ben. "You got any carpentry skills?"

"A few. Are you saying you need an extra hand?"

"We need all the hands we can get."

"Count me in," Ben said. "That's if Julie won't be in the way."

"Rachel will probably be helping with the food. Maybe she can bring Sue Ann along, then the girls won't get bored with what the rest of us are doing."

"Sounds good," Ben decided.

Loren capped Ben's shoulder. "Seems like you and Julie fit right in around here."

Yes, it seemed that he did. Yet he and Julie didn't belong here. They had a life in Vermont that was waiting for them.

Somehow, that thought was more troubling than comforting.

As Ben hammered a plank into place on Saturday, he had to admit too many of his thoughts had centered around Cassie since he'd arrived at Twin Pines almost a month ago. Dressed for a day of physical labor that he'd welcomed so he didn't think about other things, his tank shirt molded to him and he could feel the sweat dripping down his back. He tilted his hat and hammered with renewed vigor.

He'd risen at 4:00 a.m. and driven to the sight of the barn raising. Cassie planned to bring Julie as soon as she was ready. To his surprise, Julie hadn't cared that he'd left early and was looking forward to the day, playing with Sue Ann.

How she'd changed in just a few weeks. He caught sight of her now as she darted around the yard with Sue Ann, throwing a ball to the family's yellow lab.

Maybe he should get a dog. A little voice whispered, *She really wants a horse.*

That's not going to happen, he thought.

Then his gaze fell on Cassie as she rubbed elbows with a handsome neighbor. She handed a plank to him. He smiled, took it, then hammered it in place.

Ben felt a pang of jealousy that absolutely shook him. He hadn't even looked at a woman since his divorce, now here he was, jealous, wishing he could carry Cassie off to bed, worrying about what would happen when she tried to reach her father. That was, if the private investigator could find out anything. She'd been quieter since her visit to Laramie, except when she was around Julie. He wondered what kind of childhood she'd had and how she'd ended up at Twin Pines. But he'd found Cassie didn't share personal information easily, which told him she didn't trust many people. He wanted her to trust him...more than wanted her to trust him.

The morning passed quickly and sandwiches were passed around for lunch. From the activity in the kitchen and the women buzzing around, they were preparing a feast for supper.

Mid-afternoon he'd just climbed down from the roof to pull a bottle of water from the cooler when Cassie approached him with a tall plastic cup. "How about some homemade lemonade?"

The cup she was holding was full of ice as well as lemonade and was sweating in her hand. He knew he wasn't fit to be around after working on the roof, but she didn't seem to mind as she stood there holding out the cup to him.

His gaze ran from the cup to her. She'd pulled her hair back into a low ponytail. She'd gotten some sun today, too. It was evident on her cheeks, on her arms, on her neckline. He couldn't help looking, and more important, he couldn't help wanting. A hunger he barely recognized was doing a slow burn in his gut. She must have seen it in his eyes because her breaths seemed to come a little faster.

To shift his mind to something else, he quickly asked, "What are the girls up to?"

Looking relieved, Cassie smiled. "They're the smart ones. They're sitting under the cottonwood with Barker, reading Little Women. Marilyn Whittaker pulled it from her bookshelf. She'd kept it, hoping for some grandkids."

"That was her son you were talking to earlier?"

"I was talking to a lot of people, but yes, Chet and I were talking. Why?"

"I just wondered if you ever dated him."

Cassie laughed and shook her head. "Chet is a confirmed bachelor, usually out for a good time. We're neighbors and that's about it." She eyed Ben curiously, then asked, "Does it matter who I talk to, or if I dated Chet?"

He'd never known Cassie to be coy or even flirty, but her question was flirty now, and he found he liked the idea of bantering with her. "Maybe it bothers me to think about you kissing somebody else." He took the cup from her hand, took a few swallows, then watched her reaction.

"It shouldn't bother you unless—"

"Unless I was thinking about being more than friends?" He took a step closer to her and she didn't back up.

"How is that even possible?" she asked, looking fairly startled...or maybe she was just looking afraid.

"I don't know. I do know I'd like those few kisses to go a lot farther."

After a few moments, when she looked away from him over the rolling pastures to the cedars in the distance, she said, "I can't risk getting involved knowing you'll be leaving."

After studying her, he asked, "Would you risk getting involved if you knew I was staying?"

That frightened look was back in her eyes. "I don't know."

"You're going to have to let a few walls down if you want to be happy, Cassie. Since I came here, I've realized

I have to do that. Sure, it's hard after being hurt and I don't even know if you have been hurt because you don't seem to want to confide in me."

"Confide in you about what? I've told you things I wouldn't tell just anybody. Only Loren and Rachel knew how Gillian found me. And now, looking for my dad, I told you all about that."

"Yes, you did, and that's what's happening right now. But you haven't told me about what happened after your mom died or how you came to Twin Pines. Secrets are usually just painful memories. I understand that. But I'd like to know who you really are, Cassie, besides the woman who gentles horses, ropes cattle and can relate so well to my daughter."

He could see his words were affecting her. Her expression grew more vulnerable, her brown eyes shiny. There were too many people around or he'd take her into his arms. Maybe later. Maybe tonight. Maybe when they got back to Twin Pines. After all, her bedroom wasn't so far from his.

"Cassie!" someone called to her from the other side of the barn. "I hear you've got lemonade. We might be willing to pay you a quarter for a glass."

Turning away from Ben, she laughed. "It's free today, Jacob. I'll pour some more and bring it right over." Then before Ben could say another word, she gave him a look that said they were done with their conversation.

As she headed for the house, he thought—she could believe that they were finished if it would make her feel better. But it wasn't true...because he'd be bringing up the subject again.

Chapter Nine

Cassie couldn't take her eyes off of Ben whether he was hammering a new wall in place or helping to shingle the roof. In that shirt, with his summer tan, he drew her gaze to him over and over again.

Loren had filled Ben in on barn raising and the social that usually followed, so like everyone else he'd brought along a change of clothes. The men were all washing off under the spigot outside and Cassie took in Ben's naked upper body with more relish than she wanted to. She'd known he had muscles. When he'd kissed her, she'd felt them. She'd seen them in that tank he'd worn today. Although once before she'd seen him shirtless, his body was even more magnificent today. As he ran his head under the spigot and slid his fingers through his dark wet hair and straightened, she watched the play in the muscles of his back, the indentation of his spine, the width of his shoulders. One of the other men said something and he laughed.

As he turned toward the house, his black chest hair

glimmered with droplets of water and she followed the line of it down under his belt. A body tremble shivered up her spine as she remembered everything he'd said. Just what was he suggesting? That they carry on a long-distance affair? Would she be willing to do that? Looking at him now, and feeling as if he were Adam and she was Eve, it was a distinct possibility.

Darkness had fallen until all the food was served on the tables in the backyard of the house. It was a feast all right—smoked pulled-pork, ribs, roasted chicken. Side dishes were numerous, too, including baked beans, salads and vegetable casseroles. With the long hard day, everyone had ravenous appetites, except maybe for her. She'd lost hers entirely, at least any appetite for food, as she'd watched Ben wash under the spigot. Still, she pretended to push food around on her plate as she made conversation and tried to keep her eyes from meeting his across the table. But every time he cut her a glance, she felt a tingle to her boots. When she glanced at Julie sitting farther down the table with Sue Ann, she felt a kind of warmth in her heart that she'd never known before. Is this how Tina had felt about her? Is that why she had left her almost everything? Maybe you didn't have to do anything to deserve love. It just was.

Love. Had she fallen in love with Ben O'Donnell? That idea made her head spin.

He reached across the table and tapped her hand. "Are you okay?"

Her mouth was dry and she felt as if she had one of Sunny's cookie biscuits lodged in her throat. But somehow she managed to say, "I'm fine."

"You're not eating."

"Sure, I am."

"Maybe you got too much sun?"

No, not too much sun. But maybe she was drowning in sensations and feelings she didn't understand.

She just shook her head. "Really, I'm fine." Pushing her folding chair back, she stood, picked up her plate and said, "I'm going to see what the dessert table looks like."

Ben just quirked an eyebrow at her as she headed for the dessert table and chocolate cake. She needed something to calm her down.

Dessert worked just fine until music started playing, until couples started dancing on the patio, until the darkness and the lights and the chatter made the end-of-the-day celebration a party. Julie and Sue Ann wandered into the house and settled on the sofa watching a DVD while the grownups mingled outside.

Realizing she'd left her phone in her duffel when she'd changed clothes earlier—it was in the pocket of the jeans she'd worn to help with the building of the barn—she was about to go up the back porch steps to fetch it when she felt a hand on her shoulder—a very large, warm, masculine hand.

"How about a dance?" Ben asked, nodding to the patio.

"I don't dance," she responded automatically, feeling totally out of her league.

"Don't or won't?"

"I just never learned." Usually at this type of get-together she joined in square dancing, but not much else.

"That's no problem. Come on. There's really nothing to it."

Nothing to it. Being held in Ben O'Donnell's arms. Right! Nothing to it.

Tables and chairs from the patio had been set around the outskirts. A few men played horseshoes under the floodlight's glare, and Cassie heard the clink of a ringer as Ben took her into his arms.

She panicked for a moment. "I'm going to step on your feet."

He laughed and didn't seem to think much of her warning. "My boots will survive. Just try to follow my lead."

Follow his lead. Into what? Heartache and loss? More abandonment? She couldn't forget her childhood and the families who hadn't wanted her. She couldn't forget her mother dying, other people she tried to get close to moving away.

"You're thinking too much," Ben scolded. "Just relax."

No, she wasn't thinking, she was feeling. She was feeling desired and needed, and as if she wanted to crawl into his embrace and let him lead her anywhere. That was much too dangerous to even contemplate!

But Ben's hold wouldn't let her resist the exciting intoxication of being this close to him. It wouldn't let her resist breathing in his scent of hard work that still lingered. It wouldn't let her resist looking up into his eyes and getting lost in their green depths.

Oh, my gosh! She was so in trouble here. She didn't think she could call what they were doing dancing. They were swaying, and he was moving his feet now and then. Caught against him, she had no choice but to follow.

So many delicious sensations washed over her she couldn't sort them out. He was tall and strong and she felt herself leaning into him. How long had it been since she'd actually leaned on someone? All of her life she'd been fighting to be self-sufficient.

"Come with me," he murmured close to her ear, and she didn't think twice about letting him guide her around two tall pines until they were in the shadows and away from the glare of the patio lights and the chatter of the other people.

Before she had time to breathe he'd slipped his hands under her hair and tilted her face up to his. The scents of sage and pine wound about her as his lips possessed hers. His kiss asked that she hold nothing back, and she didn't.

When he broke away, she could hear his ragged breathing and she knew hers was the same. "I've been wanting to do that all day," he said.

"And I've wanted you to do it all day."

He wrapped his arms around her as if he was afraid she'd run away. That should have warned her what was coming.

"So, tell me what happened after your mom died. Where exactly did you go?"

She felt safe in Ben's arms, she really did, and she gave into that safety. "I went to a group home. It was kind of a holding place until a family would take us. Too many kids, not enough foster families."

"How long were you there?"

"About six months."

"And then?" he asked.

In the past few weeks she'd seen the admiration Ben had for her, in how she handled Julie, in how she worked, in the way she managed the ranch. She didn't want to lose any of that respect. Earning respect had been a hard-won fight. It was hard to give up even an iota of it.

So she gave him the disinfected version. "Foster families after that. Most weren't so great."

"I'm sorry you had to go through that. I'm sorry you didn't find a family like Lucy did, who wanted you and adopted you."

His compassion made her feel even worse, so she said brightly, "Tina adopted me, even though we never made it official. She became the mom and the sister that I didn't have, and a great mentor, too. She taught me everything I know."

Because she didn't want Ben to probe any further, because she didn't want to lie by omission, she leaned a little closer to him again, and he took the hint.

Bending his head, he muttered, "I feel like a teenager wanting to make out with my first girlfriend."

As his lips covered hers, any thoughts of talking vanished. They knew they didn't have long. They knew they couldn't stay hidden and away from everybody else. She almost felt desperation in Ben's kiss, and she felt the same way.

After he broke away, he gave a rough chuckle. "I'd take you to the barn so we could be alone, but it's one big, empty cavern right now."

She knew what he meant about being alone. He meant he wanted to make love to her. Or was that what he meant? Maybe he just wanted to have sex. Maybe he just wanted to act on chemistry because it had been so long since his divorce.

She had lots of questions, but she was pretty sure he didn't have the answers, either. The bond growing between them was new, never tested. What would happen when it was?

What would happen when she told him the truth?

An hour later when they were back at the ranch, Ben took Julie upstairs to put her to bed. After their make-out session they'd gone back to the patio, danced another dance and then called it a day. She could feel he wanted her. She wanted him. Should she invite him to her room? Should she lay out her whole history and then say, *Okay, now what do you think?*

Still mulling that over, she noticed the light on the answering machine was blinking. She pushed PLAY and then heard Lucy's voice. "Cassie, call me as soon as you get this. I tried to reach you on your cell phone. Where are you? Call me."

Her phone. It was still in her jeans in her duffel bag. She didn't know if she heard excitement in Lucy's voice or something much worse than that. Afraid something had happened to Zack, or maybe one of the McIntyre family, Cassie hunted for her cell phone and pressed SPEED DIAL for Lucy's number.

"Where have you been?" Lucy asked, sounding worried.

"I'm sorry. I was at the barn-raising today. I left my phone in my old pair of jeans. We just got home and I saw your message on the machine. What's going on?"

She heard Lucy let out a breath. "I forgot about the barn-raising. I heard from Gillian. She tried to reach you, too."

Cassie hadn't even bothered checking messages when she reached for her phone to call Lucy. "So, you tell me. What's going on?"

"They think they've found Walter Hunter."

Cassie was sure her heart stopped beating for at least a minute. "They think they found him?"

"They're pretty sure. He lives in Cottonwood, Arizona. He was born there. He has a shop in Sedona, which isn't that far away from Cottonwood, where he sells his wood carvings and other artisans' crafts. He has a website, too. There's a carving of a foal on it that looks very much like the one that you have."

Now Cassie's heart was beating very hard and pounding in her ears.

Ben came into the kitchen and must have seen something in her expression because he came over to stand by her and put his hand on her shoulder.

"Is there anything else?" Cassie asked, needing to know everything.

"Yes. He has a family—a wife and a daughter and a son. His daughter's eighteen and his son's sixteen. Beth and Drew. His wife's name is Olivia. She's from Cottonwood, too. Jake said apparently Mr. Hunter worked at just about everything, construction mostly, saving his money. When he settled in Cottonwood he invested it, was smart about diversifying as it accrued. Then he and his wife opened the store in Sedona. They have a good eye for marketable artists."

"How did Jake do this?"

"He used databases and public records. Gillian said he went backwards and forwards. Most of all he checked with her at each step to see if it felt right."

"So, what now?"

"I have a phone number if you want to call."

After only a heartbeat, she asked soberly, "That's what we want, isn't it?"

"I think so. Zack can't get away right now, but I can drive up tomorrow and we can do this. Jake got a cell phone number, as well as a shop and a home number, so we should be able to reach him."

"Do you want to drive here alone?"

"The weather's beautiful and I'm a very capable and self-sufficient woman, just like you are. Yes, I can come alone. We'll see what he says and then we'll decide what we're going to do next."

"That sounds like a plan."

"No expectations, Cassie."

"Right, no expectations at all." They were both denying the obvious truth. They were hoping for a miracle, a happy reunion, a chance to be connected to the man who had given them life.

After Cassie disconnected the call, it seemed the most natural thing in the world to turn into Ben's arms. He held her and rocked her back and forth. "Did Donovan come through?"

"He and Gillian did. They're certain they have the numbers and background info on the right Walter Hunter."

After Ben held her for a few more minutes, he murmured close to her ear, "Do you need to check the horses?"

She shook her head. "Loren said he'd take care of it."

Of one mind, they turned off the lights, then mounted the steps together, Ben's arm still around her.

At the door to her room, Ben kissed her again. It was a hungry kiss. His hand passed down her back and pressed her into him.

Then he reluctantly backed away, clearing his throat. "Julie fell asleep almost immediately. If she wakes up and needs me I have to be here for her."

But as he studied Cassie and she gazed back at him, he groaned, kissed her again and opened the door to her room. "Is this what you want?" he asked, as he backed her toward the bed.

"Yes." She had never wanted anything more in her life.

She reached for him, stroked his face and realized she was in love with him. Pushing aside fear and doubts, she began unbuttoning his shirt. Soon they were both naked in bed, kissing and touching, and for Cassie...loving. Was Ben loving her, too? Or was he just caught in the moment?

It didn't take long before she was caught in the moment. His kisses and caresses gave her a sense of belonging she'd never felt before. She was truly wanted. But at the last moment, Ben reached for his jeans, plucked out his wallet and pulled a condom from it. Oh yes, she wanted him to use the condom, but how long had he been prepared? Had he expected this to happen? He said he hadn't dated, but—

Doubts. So many doubts. Such a lack of trust.

But when he looked down at her, when he stroked her hair from her cheek, when he kissed her as if he'd never stop, those doubts didn't seem important at all. When they became one, she felt she found something she'd searched for all her life. She held onto him, wishing she never had to let go.

Ben awakened and gazed down at Cassie in the predawn shadows. They'd fallen asleep in each other's arms. His chest ached when he thought about how they'd come together. Had it been a mistake? He didn't know if he could ever trust another woman to stay. Julie would become devastated if she got truly attached and then something happened between him and Cassie. What were they going to do, carry on an affair long distance?

Oh, sure, he'd asked himself that question before last night, though last night, wanting Cassie had taken precedence over everything else.

She stirred and he brushed a finger over her shoulder. As she shifted to her side and looked up at him, her eyes were more vulnerable than he'd ever seen them.

"Are you okay?" he asked, his voice morning-husky.

"I am," she said with a certainly that he thought was a bit forced.

"I don't know where we go from here," he said honestly.

"I don't, either," she agreed. "Can I ask you something?"

"Sure."

"How long have you carried that condom in your wallet?"

He suspected where that question had come from. Cassie had been kicked around and abandoned, and she obviously didn't trust easily. He'd told her he hadn't dated, and that was true. He couldn't be insulted that she needed reassurance.

"It's been there since I went to town with Loren last week and stopped in a drugstore. And I know what your next question is going to be. Did I plan on last night happening? No, I didn't. I just knew something strong was brewing between us and I'd be ready if it went out of control."

"It went out of control last night."

"Yes, it did. Are you sorry about that?" Because if she had regrets, then he'd know he'd taken advantage of her. She'd been stirred up and turmoiled about the idea of calling a man she didn't know and asking him if he was her father. At first, he'd just wanted to give her comfort, but that comfort had quickly turned into desire.

"No, I'm not sorry. Are you?"

Before he could answer, his phone, holstered on the belt of his jeans, began beeping.

He thought about letting it go to voice mail, but this early in the morning it could be serious. "I'd better take that."

He grabbed the phone, checked the screen and said, "It's my VP."

"At 4:30 in the morning?"

"It's 6:30 there. East coast time, remember?" As soon as he said it, he knew he shouldn't have. The time difference was a reminder of their two different worlds and the fact that he'd be heading back to his soon.

Aware of Cassie watching him, he listened to Greg's agitated voice as he told Ben what was going on. After he'd finished explaining their problem, Ben said, "There's no way I can handle this over the phone. Digital pictures aren't going to do it, either. I need to see those samples and figure out what's wrong with them. Then we need to decide what to do about our clients. This requires a full-scale discussion. Hold on a minute."

Ben turned to Cassie. "I need to ask you a favor."

She looked puzzled. "What?"

"I need Greg to fly out here so we can put our heads together and figure out what's going on and fix it. Would it be possible for him to stay in the bunkhouse? I think he'd get a kick out of that. It would only be for one night, maybe two."

"Sure, he can stay in the bunkhouse. Or the guest cabin."

Ben grinned. "My guess is he'll choose the bunkhouse. He's game for things like that." He went back to the phone. "Greg? Catch the first flight out to Wyoming and see what a working cattle ranch is like firsthand. There's a bunkhouse bed waiting for you. Or a guest cabin. Whatever you prefer."

Greg laughed. "Are you serious?"

"Sure am, if you want to do it. Otherwise you can send the samples and we can video-conference and—"

"I'll be there as soon as I can. A working cattle ranch, huh?"

"Horses, too," Ben joked. After giving Greg details of Twin Pines' location, he clicked off.

"He's your right-hand man?" Cassie asked.

"Yep, like Loren is for you. Only Greg's younger than I am, smart as a whip, great with numbers, a good eye and a talent for marketing."

"Wow. I hope he gets a bonus each year."

Ben chuckled. "Yeah, he does."

Cassie began to slide to the other side of the bed but Ben caught her arm and pulled her back to him. After a long, lingering kiss that made him want to crawl back under the sheets with her, he rustled up some good sense, broke away and gathered his clothes. There would be time enough to think about what had happened between them last night...later.

Chapter Ten

Cassie could hardly keep from jumping out of her skin by the time Lucy arrived. She'd kept herself busy with chores. She and Ben had taken Julie on a trail ride. When she looked at him and realized she was in love with him, she practically freaked. And when she thought about what might happen after Lucy arrived, she double-freaked. Falling in love and finding a father was a little bit too much to handle in a month's time.

Had it only been a month since Ben arrived? Maybe time wasn't as important a factor as chemistry or bonds or a feeling that just couldn't be explained.

So when Lucy's SUV rolled up after lunch, Cassie was ready for anything that would lower her stress level even a little. Ben and Julie came out to greet her, too.

When he pulled her travel bag from the back seat, Lucy protested, "You don't have to do that."

"I have orders from Zack to watch over you."

"He called you?" She sounded indignant.

"Now don't pull that independent and self-sufficient act that Cassie does. Zack and I both know you're both very capable, but at a time like this it doesn't hurt to keep watch. Right?"

Lucy's indignation faded away as she looked from Cassie to Ben, and back to Cassie again. "Right," she said. "It doesn't hurt to keep watch." As Ben and Julie went up the steps into the house, Lucy bumped Cassie's elbow. "What's happened here?"

"I don't think now is a good time to get into it."

This time Lucy took hold of Cassie's elbow and didn't budge. "Spill it."

Shifting from one foot to the other, Cassie couldn't believe how uncomfortable she felt about this. "After the barn-raising yesterday, after you called last night, Ben and I spent some time together."

A smile broke across Lucy's face. "Really? That's wonderful." She looked at Cassie. "Isn't it?"

"I don't know, Luce. He doesn't know so much about me."

"So tell him. Why didn't you tell him before you, well—you know?"

"It happened fast, and I just didn't have the courage, I guess. So much is happening right now."

"You have to tell him."

"I will. But his right-hand man is coming and will be here a day or two. I just don't think now is the right time. Especially since you have to give me pointers on a couple of meals to make. Before I knew Greg was coming, I gave Rachel time off."

But Lucy wasn't distracted by the idea of Rachel

not cooking. "If you care about him, Cassie, don't keep secrets from him. Zack did that with me. Remember?"

Cassie did remember. "But everything worked out between you."

"It might have worked out sooner and saved us all a lot of heartache if Zack and I had been honest with each other about who we were and our feelings right from the beginning."

Cassie scoffed. "That's not the way relationships work and you know it. It takes time for trust to build and even then—it's just hard to reveal so much."

"So what you're saying is you don't know how he feels."

"Not exactly."

Lucy rolled her eyes. "All right. Then let's deal with one man at a time. You get on the landline, I'll get on the cordless phone and we'll make this call."

Standing in the kitchen a few minutes later, tapping her foot, Cassie's gaze locked with Lucy's. They were both holding their breath as her phone tried to connect with another all the way in Cottonwood, Arizona. They'd decided to try Walter Hunter's cell phone first.

After three rings, a deep male voice asked, "Hello?"

Cassie gave a nod to Lucy, who clicked in so she could hear the conversation, too.

"Mr. Hunter?" To Cassie's dismay her voice sounded a bit shaky.

"If you're selling coins or—"

Cassie quickly assured him, "I'm not selling anything." Then she blurted out, "My name's Cassidy Sullivan and I think I'm your daughter."

The silence that greeted her had to be filled, so she went on, "And my twin sister, Lucy, is on the line listening in too. Jeannette Sullivan was our mother. We're twenty-six years old, born on August 3, 1985. A private investigator went to a lot of trouble to try to find you for us. Please don't hang up until we figure this out."

More silence.

"Mr. Hunter, are you there?"

Finally he responded, "I went to find a chair. How do I know this isn't a scam?"

Cassie felt as if she needed a chair herself.

Lucy took over this time. "Mr. Hunter, I'm Lucy— Lucy Burke. Jeannette gave birth to twin girls. She kept Cassie, and I was given up for adoption. Cassie and I just found each other a short time ago. She has your watch."

"My watch? How can that be? When I finally landed somewhere, with decent work, I tried to find Jannie. What I found out was that she'd been killed. I used a P.I., too, and he found the notice of her death."

After a long, deep breath, Cassie plunged in again. "I was five when Mom was killed in an accident. She cherished your watch. She used to pull it out and show it to me, though she wouldn't let me play with it. The night she died, while the police and social worker were talking, I grabbed it and put it in my stuffed horse. I kept it with me all these years, not even knowing who it belonged to. I just knew it was something mom loved."

She hurried on, "We don't want anything from you, I mean nothing monetary or anything like that. I manage Twin Pines Ranch, near Cheyenne and Lucy—

she just got married and lives in Long Brush. She was raised on a ranch there. After we found each other, we just thought it would be good if we tried to find you."

"That was twenty-seven years ago," he said, his voice husky. "Jeannette and I— We were kids. I cared for her. I cared for her a lot. But I had nothing, nothing to offer her...except for that pocket watch."

"You gave it to her along with a foal. It has your name carved underneath."

"Not my first name. How the dickens did you find me?"

She couldn't tell if he was pleased about it or regretted it. "That's a really long story and we'd love to tell you all about it. In fact, we'd like to meet you."

Heavy silence weighed on the line again.

Lucy bit her lower lip and Cassie knew whatever happened next could change their lives in a big way.

"I have a family," he said. "I have a wife and two kids. They don't know anything about Jeannette. I can't just spring this on them. I can't—"

"No decisions have to be made now," Cassie told him, keeping her voice even, her good sense at the forefront. "Let me give you our contact information and our numbers. And then after you've thought about all of this, if you want to know more, if you want to get to know us, just call one of us. Or email." She looked toward Lucy and Lucy nodded. Cassie would, of course, give him Lucy's email.

She heard the scrape of a chair. She heard a rustle of paper. Then eventually he said, "Go ahead. Give me your names again and where I can reach you."

Suddenly Cassie's hope began slipping away. This wasn't the reaction either she or Lucy had been hoping for. They wanted a father who would embrace them with open arms, wholeheartedly, without any hesitation. But this was also what Gillian had warned them about. So she gave her father contact information as if she were rattling it off to a business owner.

After she'd finished, he said again, "This is a shock. I have to figure out the best thing to do...for everybody."

"We know that," Lucy assured him. "We thought about this a long while before we contacted you."

"So, did your mother speak of me to someone? Is that how you got my name?"

"We had expert people working with us. One of them has a gift for this kind of thing."

He went silent again. "All right. I have your numbers and email address. I will let you know, one way or the other, what I decide."

One way or the other? If he was going to let them into his life or shut them out?

Two minutes later, after a mumbled "It was good talking to you" and "Goodbye", Lucy and Cassie looked at each other, then reached for hugs.

Cassie never cried easily. She'd learned to hide her emotions a long time ago. Especially now, she had to be strong. She could tell Lucy had been really affected by the phone call.

"It'll be okay," Cassie murmured to her. "It will."

"It might not be," Lucy mumbled. "If he searched for love long and hard and he found it now, he's not going to want to tamper with it. We really can't fault him for that. Why jeopardize something he has for something he doesn't know about?"

Everyone had cleared out so she and Lucy could have privacy, but now Ben came into the kitchen from outside and studied them. "Are you all right?"

From their expressions, which were by no means joyous or happy, he could obviously tell the conversation hadn't been what they'd hoped for.

"He has a life and he doesn't want it tampered with?" Ben guessed.

"I think that's the problem," Cassie agreed, letting go of Lucy.

Her twin went to the counter, picked up a napkin and blew her nose. "I don't know why I'm so upset. I have a wonderful family and Cassie's part of that now. She can share my parents. It's just— Feeling rejected is the pits."

To her relief, Cassie found her equilibrium returning. "Yep, the pits. But one way or the other, we haven't lost anything, Luce. We were hoping to gain something, but instead we might just stay the same. We're okay."

Ben clasped Cassie's shoulder. "You're okay, yet it hurts knowing someone's out there you could have a connection to and they don't want it."

Cassie knew Ben was talking about his ex-wife. Did he still have feelings for her? Was he over her? But, as if he read her mind, Ben frowned. "I know what you're thinking. We'll talk about that later."

But Lucy shook her head. "No, you can talk about it now. I have to call Zack and tell him what happened. I'll go upstairs in case I start blubbering again."

"You don't have to hide what you're feeling," Cassie assured her.

Lucy gave her a weak smile and headed for the stairs.

Awkwardness settled over Ben and Cassie for a minute, until he said, "I could never get back together with Melinda. She abandoned our daughter. How can I ever forgive that?"

"But if you still have feelings for her—"

"I have regrets, not feelings. I have if-onlys and what-ifs and I wish I had handled so many things differently. But Melinda's moved on and I—" He gently caressed Cassie's cheek. "I'm beginning to."

When Ben kissed her, Cassie almost forgot about the father who might not want her. She almost forgot about secrets she was still keeping.

Almost.

It was late morning the following day when Lucy left. Ben and Julie had gone to the airport to pick up his vice-president and Cassie suddenly felt nervous as she tended to chores. She thought about dinner tonight and Ben's guest. She didn't cook much, mainly because she was afraid she'd mess up a recipe. But Lucy had told her how to make a never-fail pot-roast. This morning she'd put it in the crock pot with herbs, onions and a little bit of wine. Lucy told her by dinner it would be melt-in-your-mouth ready.

She hoped so. She did know how to steam vegetables, boil potatoes to mash and pull the cake from the freezer that Rachel had baked. So there really wasn't anything to be nervous about. It was just...

Everything seemed so up-in-the-air. She and Lucy didn't know what their dad would decide. Since Lucy had stayed in her room with her last night, she'd missed being with Ben. This morning he'd said as much and given her one of those smiles that made her forget her name. They were so new, and she didn't know what to do next with him. Ever since she'd come to live with Tina, she'd felt her life had been settled. But now everything was so unsettled again, and that put her in a tailspin.

So when Ben and Julie returned to the ranch with Greg Rayburn an hour later, she wasn't sure how to act or what to say and do.

"This is Uncle Greg," Julie said proudly, introducing Cassie to Ben's VP.

Ben's daughter seemed totally at home with him, and Cassie supposed the two men consulted a lot. Greg Rayburn had sandy blonde hair, had to be in his late twenties or early thirties, wore tortoise-shell glasses, and had an air of sophistication about him. Even in jeans and a polo shirt, she could tell he was all-city. His boots looked brand new.

She shook his hand. "I heard you want to sleep in the bunkhouse."

"I've always wanted to get a taste of bunkhouse life. Ben said you might even put me to work if I get up early enough."

"Oh, you'll be awake. Loren, Clem and Dusty don't stand on ceremony. If you're lucky, Dusty will make one of his famous omelets." She smiled and added, "If you can rustle up an appetite at 5:00 a.m."

He groaned. "So everything Ben said was true. Early to bed and early to rise."

She laughed. "And mucking out stalls, too."

After Greg glanced around the kitchen, he peeked into the living room. "Ben said you did a lot of this yourself. You have a good eye for color."

"Thanks. I know what I like, plus I do have a stash of decorating magazines."

Greg chuckled. "We'll have to get your opinion on some of our new colors and patterns."

Colors and patterns. She could deal with those. "Sure."

Ben was watching the two of them and seemed pleased with the way they were getting along.

Julie sidled up next to her. "Can I have a cookie?"

"Sure, you can. It'll be a while till supper. Do you want to come with me to the barn while your dad and Greg have a meeting?"

"What are we going to do, watch Sunny play with the other horses?"

Cassie suggested, "Maybe we'll try to put a blanket on Sunny again today."

Julie explained to Greg, "Cassie's gentling her."

"She's picking up the lingo," Greg said.

"She's turning into a cowgirl," Ben agreed. "You should see her on a horse. We rode down along the stream day before yesterday, and she had no trouble keeping up."

"My favorite horse is Buttercup," Julie informed

Greg. "She's almost white. I even rode her without a saddle one day like a real cowgirl. Are you going to go riding?"

"If your dad and I finish all our business, I guess that's a possibility."

Playing hostess, which was something that felt a bit foreign, Cassie pulled a plate from the cupboard and stacked it with cookies from the cookie jar. "Do you need to use my office?" she asked Ben.

"That probably would be best. I'll set up my computer with the printer. I might have to fax, too."

"Whatever you need to do. Take the cookies and the drinks along back with you. Julie and I will be at the barn. You have my cell phone number if you want us."

With a nod, Ben walked her and Julie to the door. Julie had almost finished her cookie, but Cassie didn't bother to take one.

He bent to her, his breath fanning her ear, as Julie went out on the porch and down the steps. "After Greg turns in, maybe you can join me in my bed tonight."

"Maybe I can," she agreed, giving him a coy smile, liking the darkening in his eyes. She hadn't flirted in a lot of years, and it was fun doing it with Ben.

While Cassie put a blanket on Sunny fifteen minutes later, she and Julie talked. At first Julie chattered about Sunny and the other horses, and how much she loved riding Buttercup. But then she ventured into more personal territory. "Mommy lives in this place that's all shiny, and silver, and black-and-white with lots of glass."

Cassie knew she had to careful, and neutral, for Julie's sake. "So it's very modern?"

"I guess. She doesn't have things sitting around. You know, things like that bowl you have in your kitchen that you said was Tina's favorite. You put fruit in it now."

"Yep, I now what you mean. And tonight we're going to be using her favorite dishes. It helps me bring back memories."

"Right. It's like Mom doesn't want any memories around. The place even has an echo."

Whenever Cassie took the rugs and the drapes out of a room, it did have a hollow emptiness and an echo. "Do you have a room when you go there?"

"Oh, yeah. It looks like the rest of the house."

"Could you decorate it the way you want?"

"I don't know. I never asked. I've only been there twice. She took me to the zoo to see all the different homes for the animals. The zoo was neat, but she just wanted to hurry through it like it was something to get done, not like it was fun doing it. Do you know what I mean? I don't like going to Seattle. I don't like staying in that house with her."

Part of the problem was that the city and her mother's condo were new to Julie. "Tell me something, honey. How did you feel when you took your first trail ride?"

"You mean out of the corral?"

"Yes. How did you feel?"

"I was happy to be there, happy to be on Buttercup, but I was worried what would happen. I was worried he would go too fast and I'd fall off. I was worried I wouldn't keep my foot in the stirrup. I was worried Daddy would get mad at something I did."

"But he doesn't get mad often."

"No, I know. But he was a lot grumpier at home than he's been since we came here. I like him here."

Cassie laughed. "And I think he likes how you are here. You're not so quiet. But back to the trail ride—that first time, it was kind of scary and you didn't know what to expect. But then what happened when you did it the second time and the third time?"

"Oh, the third time it was great. Buttercup went right where I wanted her to go. I felt like I was part of the saddle. You know what I mean?"

"Oh, I know. Between the first time and the third time you got a more comfortable fit."

"So, you're saying the next time I go be with my mom maybe I'll feel more comfortable?"

"Maybe. Or maybe you'll have to do something to make yourself more comfortable. Maybe you could ask her if you could fix up your own room, or get one thing to put in it, something like that."

"I like my room here just the way it is. That was lucky, huh?"

"I don't know how much luck went into it. I wanted the rooms upstairs to make a guest feel as if they were at home. So, I guess I succeeded."

"Do you know what I'd like?" Julie asked her.

"You'd like a horse."

"Oh, besides a horse."

"What?"

"A sister like you have. Then I wouldn't ever be afraid at night, and I'd always have somebody to talk to."

"You can talk to your dad. And while you're here, you can talk to me."

"I still didn't tell him about Sunny."

"How do you feel about that?"

"I feel like I should, but I don't want him to be mad."

Cassie knew exactly how Julie felt. She wanted to tell Ben about her inability to read, about her run-in with the law, about the kind of wild teenager she'd been. But she didn't want him to be mad, either. More than that, she didn't want him to lose respect for her.

If he did, they'd have no relationship. She was sure of it.

Chapter Eleven

As Ben carved the pot roast, he glanced at Cassie. "Thanks for helping Greg feel at home."

Everything she'd planned for dinner had worked out. Even the orange glaze on the carrots. Lucy had given her explicit directions and Cassie had followed them to the letter. The potatoes she'd whipped with the mixer had turned into buttery, frothy white clouds that looked and smelled wonderful.

"He fits right in. Anyone who can laugh at himself and appreciate a horse is good on a ranch." The men had gone for a trail ride before dinner.

Ben smiled. "That's an easy way of looking at it."

"Dinner's ready!" Cassie called into the living room and almost immediately Julie came running in, Greg soon following.

Talk around the table was fast and furious about O'Donnell Carpet and life in a bunkhouse. After a slight lull, Greg said, "Ben told me you'd like to add cabins for teenagers who need a chance."

Feeling a little disconcerted, realizing that Ben and Greg might have discussed her, Cassie said quietly, "It's a dream."

"Tell me why you think being on Twin Pines could help kids," Greg urged her.

Because he seemed truly interested, she explained, "Living on a ranch is like living in a world separate from the rest of the universe. Distractions seem to drop away. Kids in trouble are distracted by feelings they don't understand—music, TV, school, peers, adults who aren't good role models. Living someplace like this and learning to care for animals can change perspective."

"You sound as if you know from personal experience."

She shrugged. "I do. More coffee?" She certainly didn't want to get into her "personal" experience. Hopping up, she went to the coffee pot, carried it to the table and filled their cups.

"You know, if you could get a corporate sponsor, you could start this project sooner and let it expand faster."

Immediately Cassie shook her head. "No. I don't want someone else pulling the strings. If I do it, I want it to remain smaller scale...personal."

She spotted the look Ben and Greg exchanged. Had they discussed backing such a project? Or helping her find backing?

As if Ben realized she was uncomfortable with the idea and maybe the conversation, he said, "Greg's flying out tomorrow morning. We managed to solve all of our problems this afternoon."

"You hardly got a taste of Wyoming," Cassie protested.

"Enough of a taste that I'd like to see more," he assured her. "Maybe when Ben comes back to Vermont, I'll take a vacation and become a real cowhand."

When Ben frowned, Cassie laughed. She couldn't quite see Greg as a cowhand. But who knew?

An hour later, as Ben put Julie to bed, Cassie went to the barn for one last nightly check. When she returned to the house, Greg had spread paperwork, sample books and some actual patches of carpet across the coffee table.

Descending the stairs, Ben stopped when he saw her. Their gazes locked and excitement and longing swept through her body. She wanted to dive right into his arms and let him carry her off to bed. But, of course, they couldn't do that until Greg went to the bunkhouse for the night.

Ben motioned to the spread on the coffee table. "Greg wants your input on new colors and designs. He thinks a woman's perspective would be valuable."

The papers with their print made her nervous. "I don't know anything about—"

Greg jumped right in. "You don't need to. I just want a gut reaction different from mine and Ben's. Consider yourself part of my focus group."

A gut reaction. She could do that.

Taking a seat in the comfy wide leather chair across from the sofa, Ben waited for her to perch beside Greg on the couch. She ran the pads of her fingers over the carpet samples. "I like the diamond pattern and this figure 8 design."

"It's the infinity symbol," Greg explained, nodding. "That's one of my favorites, too. But how do you think it looks in the two-tone rather than the solid color?"

After studying them both, she shrugged. "I like the two-tone. The pattern isn't as obvious. My guess is in a room-size piece, from a perspective farther away, it would look entirely different than it does here."

Again Greg nodded. "Ben was right. You do have a good eye for this. So tell me, what do you think the in colors are going to be?" He produced a color palette.

Unable to decipher the name of each color, she figured that didn't seem to be necessary to give an opinion. Concentrating, she finally tapped a few on his color wheel. "I don't know about in colors, but anything that has natural tones, that you could find in the scenery around you, has to be long lasting, right?"

After a chuckle and another glance at Ben, Greg responded, "Our view exactly! Lime green might be great for a year, but after that—" He shrugged. "Who can or would go to the expense of tearing up carpet after a year? Not your ordinary customer."

Pulling a glossy flyer from the bottom of the stack, he flattened it in front of her. "So this is our ad campaign. Do you think it will catch a woman's eye? Women are usually the ones who go carpet shopping."

To Cassie's dismay, there were only a few pictures on the flyer. Most of it was print. Her heart bucked, and she swallowed hard. After pretending to study it, she said, "It looks good."

That apparently wasn't enough for Greg. "It's not just the looks of it. Or the colors. What do you think of the copy? One of my ad people thought it was too formal and not friendly enough."

She couldn't read the paragraphs under the photos.

Normally she could pick out a word or two. But when she was stressed, letters just ran together and blurred, almost dancing on the page. She couldn't even begin to do this. She shouldn't have even started.

Up until now, she and Ben had spent most of their time outside. Comfortable everywhere on the ranch, she knew what the signs said. She could recognize the feed labels. The medicine for the animals was arranged in the cabinet a certain way so she knew exactly which bottle was which. Here in the house with papers and text in front of her, she felt humiliated and inadequate, dysfunctional and backward—all the terrible feelings that had plagued her during her whole life until she'd come to live at Twin Pines. Now she realized she'd begun a relationship with Ben under false pretenses, and that had been wrong.

Ben and Greg were staring at her and she was starting to sweat. Suddenly she stood, said, "I think I'm feeling a little queasy. I'm going to get some fresh air." Before either of the men could make a comment, she fled the room, ran through the kitchen and out the back door.

She'd only reached the porch when she heard the storm door open and close behind her. Then Ben was clasping her shoulder, keeping her from galloping down the steps away from him.

His voice was deep and vibrating in the dark night. "You can't read, can you?"

Whether he meant it to be or not, his question sounded like an accusation. His words were a judgment of who she was, what she did, and how she did it. She remained silent, regretting the fact she had to face him, knowing she couldn't run to the barn and hide.

"I finally put it all together in there. You depend on Loren for all the computer work. You didn't even want to think about learning a new program, even though it would have made your bookwork so much easier. You let him handle the mail, which I thought was odd. Your office is bare except for the documents Loren works with. Maybe you page through decorating magazines, but there's not another scrap of reading material anywhere. Cassie, why didn't you tell me?"

Ben sounded a little outraged, shocked, maybe even betrayed. She wasn't sure which one of them to address. All of them had to do with his reaction, not how she was feeling at being discovered, at being forced to admit her failings. She felt hurt he hadn't asked how it had happened...how she'd survived...how she handled daily life. She was hurt he didn't care about her embarrassment in front of his colleague or how she'd handle Julie when his little girl found out her secret. Most of all, she was hurt she'd made herself vulnerable to him by loving him and yet she didn't know how he felt in return.

Hearing the edge of exasperation, anger, and disbelief in his voice, she felt as if the bottom had dropped out of her world. Maybe not the bottom...just the new dreams.

"I slipped through the cracks," she explained, wanting to answer his question, yet knowing he couldn't understand unless he knew her history. "I went to kindergarten shortly after mom died and I couldn't concentrate on much, I guess. I was in the group home then. I always loved pictures but I could never figure out words. The teachers just thought I was slow—at least, that's how they labeled me. They put me on the bottom of their list and didn't spend much time with me. One year passed into the next. One foster home passed into another. The people I stayed with didn't care if I got my homework done. I threw away the notes teachers sent home. After all, I didn't want to get into trouble. What did it matter anyway? By the time I reached high school, I was truant. The thing was...nobody seemed to see...or to care."

One thing she'd always liked about Ben was his perception where she was concerned. But now she wasn't so sure about that as he asked more gently, "So what happened to change your life? Obviously something did."

All her life she'd felt that something was wrong with her...that she should have figured out how to get her feet under her sooner. But she hadn't, and she knew she had to tell him the rest. "The last foster home I was in...well, the husband was creepy. The couple didn't have kids. They mainly took me in so I could do everything they didn't want to do—cleaning, cooking mostly frozen meals, yard work. They both worked. The wife worked more hours than her husband and sometimes didn't get home until very late."

Stopping, she just wanted to skip the rest. But that's what had sent her here. "I'd stick dinner in the microwave and have it with Mr. Cromwell when I couldn't escape to my room. As the days went by, he started getting a little...too friendly. I began locking my door at night. One night after supper, he made a pass. I ran out.

Then I circled back, hot-wired his car, and took off out of Laramie. I didn't know exactly where I was headed or how far I'd get. I was going to ditch the car in Cheyenne and figure out what to do from there. But the roads were icy that night. Outside of Cheyenne, I was in an accident—a pretty serious one. Social workers got involved. And then Tina Christopher stepped in like the fairy godmother I'd never had...like the guardian angel I'd always needed. Somehow she got any charges against me dropped. My guess is that she threatened to go public with what had happened. I don't know. I only know that once she brought me to Twin Pines, it felt like home. When I met her, I looked into her eyes and I knew she was a kind person. I knew I'd finally found someone with the same qualities my mom had. Tina told me if I worked hard, I could become anything I wanted. But all I wanted was her approval. All I wanted was to learn about and take care of her horses, the cattle and the ranch. I learned so much more."

"Cassie, I'm so sorry."

Yes, he was. She could see that. But she could also see something she didn't want to see in Ben's eyes—pity. He pitied her! That was worse than anger or disapproval. She didn't want pity, especially not from him. She'd survived, found a life and was doing just fine.

He looked as if he wanted to comfort her in some way...to make up for all she'd gone through. But only one thing could do that. She needed to see respect back in his eyes. She needed him to still see her as an equal.

When he asked, "Tina knew you couldn't read?" Cassie realized he didn't.

"It didn't take Tina long to figure it out. But she said I had to want a high school diploma. I had to want to figure out how words made sense. I didn't need to do that here."

"I understand why she let you be. But especially after she died— You might have escaped juvie, but you've created a closed world for yourself here. Why wouldn't you want to learn to read?"

How could she make him understand? "A deaf person who's never heard music doesn't know what he's missing. A blind person who's never seen color, doesn't miss it. I had what I'd been searching for after my mother died—a safe place and people who cared about me. Why would I need more?"

She couldn't decipher Ben's expression. Under the glow of the porch light she could see the nerve in his jaw work and she understood he was trying to figure out how to convince her to change her life. He'd be disappointed in her if she didn't.

How could a man like Ben O'Donnell ever have feelings for a cowgirl who had never graduated from high school? Who couldn't put letters together to form words? Who didn't care about life beyond this ranch?

All she could think to say was, "You'll never understand."

She couldn't look at him anymore...and wish everything had been different...see the death of even more dreams. A sense of loneliness and isolation fell on her again. Those were feelings that hadn't haunted her for so long.

Spinning away from him, she ran down the porch steps and across the lane to the barn. She didn't look back when he called her name.

Chapter Twelve

As Ben drove Greg to the airport, neither man had anything to say. At least that's what Ben thought until Greg commented casually, "So there's something going on with you and Cassie?"

Ben cut him a glance but didn't respond.

"It's about time."

Knowing he needed to cut this conversation short, he said, "I'm not over my divorce. It's still too soon—"

"To move on? To make a new life, a different life for you and Julie?"

After a moment of quiet, Ben said tersely, "It's because of Julie I can't just jump into anything."

"Julie seems attached to Cassie."

"That's why we have to leave. I made that decision last night?"

"Because Cassie can't read?"

Last night Ben had handled everything all wrong. But he'd been shocked by Cassie's revelation. He'd also felt foolish that he hadn't caught on sooner. Wrapped up in the chemistry between them, he'd been blind to everything else. Except how Cassie and Julie had bonded. Still... Why hadn't Cassie trusted him enough to tell him? As intimate as they'd been...as passionate...as vulnerable. At least he'd felt vulnerable.

"No, not because Cassie can't read," he answered tersely, feeling as if his decision to leave was the wrong one, yet not knowing what else to do. "It's just time, that's all. My life and work are in Vermont!"

"You haven't thought about changing that?"

"Not for a woman who keeps secrets," he blurted out, giving Greg the real root of the problem. "Melinda kept secrets and look where that got us. If I had known she was as driven as she was, that nothing would get in her way, not even her daughter, I never would have married her." The bitterness and resentment he hid for Julie's sake still gnawed at him.

Greg waited a beat before asking, "What secrets did she keep?"

Never telling anyone, because telling would make him feel more of a failure, he finally admitted, "Before she left, she spilled everything. She told me she'd been unhappy for years. She admitted connecting with other men at work, telling me she was working late when she was having drinks with them or God knows what else, believing she was never meant to be a mother, convincing me our marriage had been a sham. Oh, I knew she'd pulled away. I knew sex was..." He gripped the steering wheel tighter. "A duty for both of us."

He studied the road ahead with more concentration than was necessary. "So why would I ever want to think about getting married again?"

"I didn't say anything about marriage," Greg reminded him. "I just said you should move on." He paused. "But you are the marrying kind. You're a one-woman man."

"I've had enough of this conversation," he muttered.

"Do you care about Cassie?"

Apparently he'd had enough, but his friend hadn't. "I'm confused about Cassie. We got close, Greg. So how could she have kept so much hidden from me?" There was pain in his voice and this time, he didn't care if Greg heard it.

A stretch of road peeled by.

"You're right," Greg finally responded. "Melinda kept secrets. It sounds as if she was dishonest about a lot. But do you think Cassie's dishonest? Or do you think she was just afraid your reaction would be exactly what it was? My guess is she's known a lot of rejection and felt even more judgment."

If Greg was right, that wasn't something he could fix now. If what he'd said had hurt Cassie deeply, she'd never forgive him. It was a mess the whole way around. And the only way he knew of keeping Julie safe from getting hurt was to leave before she bonded even more deeply with Cassie.

All Ben could think about as he drove back to Twin Pines was that he and Julie had to leave quickly. This trip had done them both a world of good. But now it was time to go home. Except the idea of going home felt...empty.

It didn't take much of a search for him to find Cassie and Julie in a corner of the barn, sitting on bales of hay. Both had a napping cat on their laps. They were talking and, out of sight, he stopped to listen.

"Somebody could teach you how to figure out letters and numbers," Julie was telling Cassie, a most serious expression on her face. "There are good teachers at my school."

Apparently Cassie had revealed her problem to Julie and they were discussing it.

He watched as Cassie laid a gentle hand on Julie's head and stroked her hair. "I don't know, honey. Since I'm older, it might be a lot harder for me to learn."

With a frown, Julie thought about that. "You sometimes teach older horses new things, don't you?"

"Sometimes. But habits are hard to break."

"But you could try to learn, couldn't you?"

Deciding this conversation was too personal for him to be eavesdropping on, Ben rustled his boot against a hay bale and both Julie and Cassie looked up.

He smiled at his daughter, though it was the last thing he felt like doing. "Honey, can you check to see if the water trough is filled?"

"Okay. If it isn't I'll turn on the spigot for a little while. C'mon, Tiger, you come with me," she said to the cat. As Julie scampered across the barn to the door, the yellow tabby followed her.

Rising from the bale, Cassie approached Ben, looking wary. "Greg's on his way back?"

"Yes. And..." There was no easy way to say it. "I think it would be a good idea if Julie and I left, too. While I was at the airport, I made reservations for us for tomorrow."

"Tomorrow? That soon?"

"I think it's best, don't you?"

The yellow tabby ran down the walkway toward them and jumped up onto a stall gate. Ignoring the cat, Ben felt an ache in his chest that he attributed to lack of sleep, chopping wood, anything but the emotions swirling inside him.

Cassie looked dismayed for a moment. But then her chin went up, her eyes grew flat, and she said in a cool voice, "You have to do what's best for you. If that's leaving, then leave. I knew you would. After all, you have a life in Vermont."

He took a step closer to her. "Cassie—"

She crossed her arms over her chest. "You don't have to say anything else. I understand why you want to take Julie home sooner rather than later."

Although Cassie was acting as if she didn't care, he wondered if she really didn't. Had the time they'd spent together mattered to her? He suddenly realized how much it had mattered to him. Still, he couldn't give in to something so new, to something that might bring a repeat of the heartache he'd experienced in his marriage. "I have to get Julie settled back in Vermont before school starts again. She needs stability and routine and everyday life."

"I thought that's what you were trying to escape," Cassie said matter-of-factly. "She was unhappy in your routine, wasn't she?"

Cassie's challenge made him defensive. "She was unhappy because her mother left and didn't want her."

"That hasn't changed."

"No. But I think we've both gotten a better perspective on all of it."

"Really? Do you know she's afraid to go to your ex-wife's house? She's afraid Melinda won't want her. She's afraid when she gets back you might not be there."

"When did she tell you that?"

"Look, Ben. She told me a lot of things, things she should be telling you. Maybe she doesn't because she's afraid you'll disapprove."

"What else hasn't she told me?" Cassie was hinting around at something and she might as well tell him whatever it was.

But she answered, "Nothing important. Just something she needs to get off her chest. We all keep secrets, Ben. We do it to protect ourselves from getting hurt. "

Suddenly a loud male voice sailed through an open stall door. "Cassie! Ben! Come quick. Julie opened the gate, took Buttercup over to the fence and climbed on before I knew what she was up to. She rode off toward the north pasture. The stream's over that way and you know how Buttercup likes to go sloshing through—"

"She's never going to be able to stay on without a saddle," Ben said, rushing outside with Cassie.

"She rode bareback for a little the other day," she reminded him. "She might be okay."

Ben had okayed that ride around the corral, knowing Cassie would never let his daughter fall. But Julie doing it on her own...

Cassie didn't hesitate to cluck to a chestnut in the corral. She grabbed the horse's lead and hiked herself onto his back. "Saddle up with Loren," she called to Ben. "Loren knows where Buttercup likes to go."

Ten minutes later, Ben's heart was in his throat as he urged his horse ahead of Loren's. He let instinct guide him as well as a plume of dust he glimpsed now and then from Cassie's horse. Mere minutes later, he pulled his horse up short.

Jumping from the saddle, he ran to Cassie and Julie who were huddled on the ground. Buttercup was standing in the stream, nosing the grass along the edge.

He dropped to the ground beside Julie. "Are you hurt?"

She was holding her arm and tears were flowing down her cheeks. "I don't want to go home, Daddy! I don't want to."

"She fell off when Buttercup veered toward the stream," Cassie explained. "From what I can tell, she chased Tiger into the barn, hoping to carry her back out and shut the door. But she heard us talking."

Apparently Julie had overheard that he'd booked tickets to fly home. But again she'd told Cassie what had happened. His daughter was staring up at him as if he'd disapprove of her again. Had his concern for her been coming across as disapproval? Was that possible?

Settling on the ground beside her, he asked gently, "Does anything besides your arm hurt?"

Julie shook her head.

He tenderly brushed dust from her cheek. "Can you tell me why you rode away?"

Staring up at him with huge green eyes, she said with a certainty that broke his heart, "You'll be mad."

With a cold splash of reality, he realized he needed a lighter touch with Julie. Building his company from scratch, he'd become matter-of-fact, stoic, even hard at times when he had to make tough decisions, negotiate contracts, fire employees who weren't towing the line. Maybe too much of that had spilled over into his personal life. Maybe walking in someone else's shoes had become foreign to him. Maybe his divorce had added protective armor that had prevented more pain but had also prevented him from really communicating with Julie.

Cupping her chin, he said quietly but firmly, "I won't be mad. I promise."

She still hesitated but finally revealed, "I thought I could ride away and hide. If you couldn't find me, then we'd miss our plane tomorrow and we could stay longer." She glanced at Cassie. "You want us to stay longer, don't you?"

Cassie took a moment before she answered and Ben guessed why. Her eyes were shiny. "I want you to stay as long as you want to. But you have to listen to what your dad thinks is best. We can't always have what we want."

"Like you didn't want your mom to die?"

"That's right."

"Like you wanted to be adopted but you weren't?"

"Right again. But then something even better happened. I came to Twin Pines and loved it here. So when you go back home, something really good can happen there, too."

Cassie and his daughter must have had some talk earlier! And he realized he was grateful Cassie understood Julie so well. He was grateful she seemed to love Julie. He was grateful for so much more. But not just grateful.

One of the ranch's four-wheel-drive pick-ups came rumbling across the pasture with Clem behind the wheel.

"I called him," Loren said from a few feet away.

Ben had forgotten he was there.

"In case Julie's arm is broken," Loren added, "I didn't think you'd want her bouncing around on a horse again. You'd better drive her to the urgent care center and have her looked at."

"Can Cassie come, too?" Julie asked.

At this moment, Ben wouldn't deny his daughter anything. But besides that, he wanted Cassie with them. When he'd seen her cradling his little girl, he'd felt as if his life had finally clicked into place. He'd felt connected. He'd felt as if Cassie completely understood what a gift Julie was and she was a woman who knew how to cherish that gift...she was a woman who knew how to cherish. He needed her beside him as they took Julie to the medical center for more than one reason. Yeah, maybe he'd botched up everything last night and this morning, too. But just maybe he could learn from his mistakes. Just maybe Cassie could forgive his stupidity and give him another chance...give them both a second chance.

Cassie's heart hurt as she drove to the medical center with Ben and Julie, as they waited for the result of the x-rays, as the doctor told them Julie had badly sprained and bruised her arm, not broken it. He put it in a sling and told them he could check it again in a few days.

Cassie knew Ben would have it checked again to make sure Julie was okay to fly. He wouldn't take any chances with his daughter because she was his life.

Julie had changed Cassie's perspective on her life. If she wanted to have children some day, and she did, then she needed to learn how to read. She needed to earn her GED. She needed to make her world broader than Twin Pines Ranch. As Julie had said, she could try.

Maybe if she concentrated on learning how to read, she could forget about Ben and Julie after they left. Maybe she could forget how she'd felt desired and safe in Ben's arms. She could forget how his opinion of her changed when he'd learned she couldn't read.

On the return drive to the ranch, they were all quiet. It had been an emotional day that had weighed on them all. At Twin Pines, she and Ben settled Julie on the sofa with a DVD and a glass of lemonade.

Then Ben asked Cassie, "Can I talk to you in your office."

He wanted privacy and she wasn't even going to guess why. She just had to get through the conversation and the next few days and then he'd be gone.

But in her office, he closed the door almost the whole way. For once, she couldn't gauge his mood. If she didn't know better, she would call his expression uncertain. Not Ben.

He began by taking a step closer to her. "I have a lot to say to you and I don't know where to start."

"Ben, if you think I shouldn't have told Julie about my background, I'm sorry."

"You have nothing to be sorry for. I'm the one who's sorry—for being arrogant and blind."

His words hit her hard and she blinked, not understanding.

"While you were getting the lemonade, Julie told me about Sunny—how she let her out."

"I didn't feel I could break her confidence. Maybe it's something else I should have told you—"

But Ben was shaking his head and stepping closer still. "If I had been the type of father I should have been, she would have told me. If I had been the type of man I should have been, you would have told me your secrets, too."

"Ben—"

He covered her lips with his fingers and his touch felt so right that she forgot to protest.

"After I met you and then after the night we spent together, I was filled with so many doubts. How could I ever trust a woman again to make vows and keep them? How could I make another marriage work? How could I keep my first one from tainting another? I didn't understand until this afternoon how I'd grown hard and inflexible, how my attitude affected Julie. She trusted you practically from the start. Why? Because you're full of understanding and compassion, not rules and fixed routines and judgment."

She really didn't know where Ben was going with this, but a tiny flicker of hope sparked and she couldn't blow it out.

"You're different from any woman I've ever known. You're freer and kinder and so passionate that I felt totally lost in you. I didn't know how to handle that. But I've got to start living again rather than avoiding risks. I've got to start loving again instead of protecting myself and Julie."

"You've been doing a lot of thinking," she said, her heart racing so fast she could hardly breathe.

"Yes, I have. I was an idiot last night. I was thinking about myself instead of you. I was hurt you hadn't confided in me. But now I understand why you couldn't. You didn't know how I felt. Maybe I didn't, either. But I'll tell you right now Cassidy Sullivan, I love you just the way you are. If you want to learn to read, we'll find the best teacher. But if you don't, that's okay, too. What's important right now, is that we be together. I can't promise to learn how to be the best dad and the best husband overnight. But I do know how to promise to try. My headquarters can be anywhere, as long as I have good people like Greg working for me. So I guess my question is—do you need an extra cowboy on Twin Pines? And...an even more important question is—will you marry me?"

She was awesomely shocked until she looked into Ben's eyes and remembered every day since he and Julie had arrived. Their bond had been growing since the moment they'd met. Still, she had to be sure... "I might never learn how to read. Your world is so different from mine."

He enfolded her into his arms. "I like your world. We'll combine the two. And whether you can learn to read or not, you're still the most courageous and kind person I know. And I love you."

She could see he meant everything he was saying. Wrapping her arms around his neck, she declared, "I love you, too, Ben. So much. Yes, I'll marry you!"

Ben's lips captured hers and swept her away to that place where dreams do come true.

Chapter Thirteen

July passed so quickly, Cassie didn't know where the days went. She'd never been so gloriously happy! When she and Ben had told Julie they were getting married, she'd just grinned and said, "Good!"

Julie had found the life she'd wanted this summer and so had Ben. At night Cassie and Ben had long discussions about when they should get married. They decided to wait until Thanksgiving. The holiday seemed appropriate.

At the end of August, Julie started school. She was in the same class as Sue Ann and didn't seem to have a problem adjusting. When Cassie and Ben attended their first parent-teacher open house together, they easily mingled with the other parents. Cassie had found her own adult literacy teacher through the school district. After some testing, she'd realized why it was hard for her to learn and strategies to adjust to her difficulties. She was making progress. Ben never hesitated to tell her how proud he was of her. At night when they made love, she knew he cherished her already. As they worked side by side many days, she realized their respect for one another was one of the first bonds they'd developed.

It was a Thursday afternoon in late September when a van lumbered up the Twin Pines lane and parked in front of the ranch house. Ben had just returned from moving cattle with Loren. He'd come inside, whirled Cassie into his arms and given her a resounding kiss. He'd just scooped her into his arms ready to carry her off to their bedroom, when there was a knock at the door.

"Maybe it's something Loren ordered. The delivery man will leave it on the porch."

But the delivery man didn't leave it on the porch. The knocking at the door became more forceful.

"I suppose we'd better get that," Ben said with a wry smile, reluctantly setting her on the floor.

She gave him a quick kiss and went to answer it.

When she opened the door, she found an older man, late forties or early fifties, with his long brown hair laced with silver tied back with leather band. He wore a serious expression and she didn't see any packages in his hands.

"Can I help you?" she asked.

"Are you Cassidy Sullivan?"

Ben crossed to her now to stand protectively beside her. "Who wants to know?"

The man looked Ben up and down then gave them an uncertain smile. "I'm Walt Hunter."

Cassie felt her knees wobble. Ben must have suspected her shakiness because he wrapped his arm around her waist.

Taking a deep breath, she tried to compose herself. She reached for the handle of the storm door to open it. "Come in!"

When her father stepped inside, she motioned to the chairs at the table. "Please sit down. Would you like coffee...soda?"

"Coffee would be great. I've been on the road for the past week—a buying trip for the store. Lots of artists out there. I try to find unique but marketable crafts."

They all knew he was trying to make conversation but Cassie couldn't seem to find the words to help him. She just wanted to look at him.

Ben asked the question she wanted an answer to. "Why didn't you call to tell Cassie you were on the way?"

Her father took a moment, then said honestly, "I didn't know if I'd head over this way. I didn't know for sure if I would stop by."

"But you did," Cassie said. "So you wanted to see me."

"I couldn't stay away," he admitted. He looked down at the table. "I told my family about you and Lucy a couple of weeks ago."

"You waited a while." Ben filled the coffee carafe with water and gestured for Cassie to sit with her dad at the table.

"I did. I needed to think on it," he responded a bit defensively.

"I'm sure my call was a shock," Cassie said with understanding. "And coming here unannounced, you could check on what I'd told you."

He looked a bit sheepish. "That's right. In fact that part was my son's idea."

"So how did your family react when you told them?" Cassie wanted to know.

"Better than I expected. I mean, my wife's a good woman and my kids are great. But I didn't want them to feel threatened in any way—like anything could ever come between us."

"And two daughters could. But Lucy and I would never do that. As we told you, Lucy's adoptive family is wonderful. Her husband is tops, too. As for me, well, Twin Pines is my home and Ben's now, too."

Ben came to her and dropped a hand on her shoulder. "I have a daughter and when Cassie and I marry at Thanksgiving, she'll be a mom to Julie."

"Thanksgiving?"

They nodded.

"How long can you stay?" Cassie asked.

"Just a day or two. I really have to get back. I just made reservations for tonight..."

"I have a guest cabin where you can stay if you'd like. And I want to call Lucy. Maybe she can drive here so she can see you, too. Is that all right?"

"That's fine. I'll stay until she can get here."

Shoring up her courage, knowing she had to continue to make some of the first moves, she reached across the table and laid her hand on top of her father's. "Thank you for coming."

When he turned his hand palm upward and clasped hers, she knew everything would be okay. She and Lucy had found their father...and he had found them.

Epilogue

Lucy had already started down the aisle in a blue velvet gown when Julie gave Cassie a hug. "We're going to be married soon!"

"Yes, we are." Cassie hugged her back. "Just as soon as you scatter those rose petals, we'll get started.

"You look beautiful!" Julie said.

"Yes, she does," Walt Hunter agreed from his position beside her.

Cassie felt beautiful in her lacy, western-cut gown with it's fringed sleeves and flounced train. But hearing her dad say it meant the world to her. Her eyes misted over as she kissed Julie's cheek, straightened and watched her daughter-to-be keep step to the rhythm of the wedding march as she walked down the aisle.

"Ready?" her father asked.

"Ready," Cassie said. She'd expected to ask Loren to walk her down the aisle. But when she'd invited her dad and his family to the wedding, he'd offered. Ben said that worked out perfectly because then he could ask his uncle to be his best man!

As her father guided her down the aisle, Cassie spotted his family. She'd met them day before yesterday when they'd arrived. She hadn't known what to expect. But her dad's wife Olivia was warm and friendly and got along famously with Rachel. His children, Drew and Beth seemed to like being around the animals. They'd gone for a trail ride with her yesterday and talked about their life in Cottonwood until Cassie felt she was really getting to know them.

Greg had flown in, too. Along with Clem and Dusty, Rachel, Sue Ann the McIntyre clan and other friends from town, Cassie felt good will and warm wishes all around her.

Julie stepped into the front pew where Zack stood while Lucy waited for Cassie so she could hold her bouquet.

When Cassie and her father reached the steps where Ben and the minister waited, Cassie's gaze met her husband-to-be's. He smiled and it was like an embrace.

Lucy took her bouquet from her, gave her a hug and a kiss, saying, "I love you. Go get married."

Holding back tears was tough as her father kissed her on the cheek and then settled her hand in Ben's. Ben thanked him, tucked her fingers into the crook of his arm and faced the minister with her.

But before the reverend began the wedding ceremony, Ben said, "You are so beautiful. I love you."

Cassie leaned close to him. "I love you, too."

The minister began, "Dearly Beloved, we are gathered together on this Thanksgiving Day—"

Ben's gaze held Cassie's as they joyously promised each other their hearts and their lives...forever after.

KAREN ROSE SMITH BOOKS
AVAILABLE IN E-BOOK FORMAT

SEARCH FOR LOVE Series
Nathan's Vow, Book 1 *
Jake's Bride, Book 2 *
Always Devoted, Book 3 *
Always Her Cowboy, Book 4 *
Heartfire, Book 5
Cassidy's Cowboy, Book 6 *
Her Sister, Book 7 *

FOREVER LOVE Series
April's Promise *

FINDING MR. RIGHT Series
Kit and Kisses, Book 1 *
Forever After, Book 2 *
When Mom Meets Dad, Book 3 *
Falling For Her Boss, Book 4 *
Toys and Baby Wishes, Book 5 *
Love in Bloom, Book 6
Ribbons and Rainbows, Book 7 *
Wish on the Moon, Book 8 *
A Man Worth Loving, Book 9 *

EVERYDAY LOVE Short Story Series
Everyday Cinderellas, Vol. 1
Everyday Prince Charming, Vol. 2
Everyday Romance, Vol.3

Garden of Fantasy
Abigail and Mistletoe
Writing is a Business

SCIENCE FICTION
SHORT STORY COLLECTION
Journey Into Chaos

BOXED SETS
Finding Mr. Right Box Set One
Finding Mr. Right Boxed Set Two
Search For Love Boxed Set One
Search For Love Boxed Set Two
Everyday Love Boxed Set

*Also available as an audio book

Excerpt from HER SISTER
Search For Love series, Book 7

Prologue

*W*here *is Lynnie? Where did she go?*
In her mind, five-year-old Clare Thaddeus called to her little sister—*Come back, Lynnie. Please come back.*

The huge policeman crouched down in front of Clare's mother at the sofa and said in a deep, slow voice, "Mrs. Thaddeus, I know you're terribly upset. But I need details. We've got an hour before daylight. If your daughter wandered outside—"

Clare's father, who'd been talking to another man in blue, glanced at her, and Clare huddled down deeper into the big green armchair. Her dad didn't come to her but rather went to her mom, sank down beside her and wrapped his arm around her. Then he spoke to the officer. "Our daughter, Lynnie, is three. She would never go outside into the dark on her own."

"Tell us again where you were last night," the policeman demanded in a not-so-nice voice.

"I worked late, preparing a brief."

"Until five a.m.?"

"Yes, until five a.m. As I told you, I always check the girls' rooms before turning in. Lynnie wasn't in her bed. I woke my wife. We looked through the whole house and then we called you."

Clare had been sleeping in her brand new room. They'd moved in here—she studied her hand and counted her fingers—five days ago. Boxes were still stacked down here and upstairs. The house was okay. There were more rooms for her and Lynnie to play hide and seek. But she didn't like being alone in her own room at night. She'd liked it better when she and Lynnie had slept in the same room.

Earlier she'd thought she'd heard Lynnie's door open...thought her sister was going to the bathroom and might come in and crawl into bed with her. But she'd been *so* sleepy. She and Lynnie had been running through the hose sprayer all afternoon in the backyard while Mommy unpacked. She was supposed to watch her sister. She was always supposed to look out for Lynnie. That's what big sisters did.

Where had Lynnie gone?

Then Clare remembered the blue car that had driven down the alley in back of the yard lots of times. The man had stopped once and watched them. But she'd thought he might be one of their new neighbors who just wanted to say hi.

Should she tell the policeman?

He was so big, and he looked mad. Her dad looked mad, too, as he asked, "Why do you want to question me and my wife separately?"

"That's just the way we do it, Mr. Thaddeus."

Although she was scared of the two big men in blue uniforms, she knew her mommy and daddy wouldn't let them hurt her. Policemen helped, didn't they? They were going to help find Lynnie.

She slipped off of the chair, went over to the sofa and tugged on her mother's arm. "Mommy, when I was playing—"

The doorbell rang.

"Are you expecting someone?" the policeman asked, his brows arched.

Not sounding at all like herself, her mother answered, "I called a friend."

"Before or after you called us?"

Her mother's face turned red. "*After*, of course."

"Mommy." She tugged on her mother's arm again while one of the policemen went to the door.

Her mother took Clare's hand. "Not now, honey. Natalie's going to take care of you for a little while so we can talk to the officers."

"But, Mommy—"

Her mom's best friend, Natalie Barlow, rushed into the living room looking as upset as her mom and dad. "What can I do?"

Her father answered quickly. "Can you take Clare upstairs? And can you call our old neighbors? Maybe they'll help search. I've got to get out there looking, but I have to finish answering questions first."

Natalie gave Clare a weak smile and took her hand. "Come on, honey. Let's go upstairs for a while."

Her mom kissed her.

Her dad gave her a nod.

She tried again. "When I was playing with Lynnie—"

Tears fell down her mom's cheeks. Her dad said, "Not now. Go upstairs with Natalie."

What she had to say wasn't important. The man in the blue car didn't matter. Only Lynnie mattered.

As Clare followed Natalie upstairs, she got very afraid. What if the policemen couldn't find Lynnie? Is that why her mommy was crying? Because she didn't think they could? Was that why her dad was mad?

Natalie bent down to her. "I don't want you to worry. Everything's going to be all right."

But Clare knew better. If Lynnie didn't come home, nothing would ever be right again.

Chapter One

"I'm not taking it back. I bought it with my own money." Shara Thaddeus stared at her mother defiantly, standing her ground. At sixteen, she was Clare's payback for the trouble Clare had given her parents when she was sixteen, though certainly not for the same reason.

At thirty-two and a single parent, Clare didn't know what to do with Shara any more than her parents had known what to do with her. She'd rebelled because she'd wanted their attention. *Any* of their attention. All of their attention. When Lynnie had been around, Clare had loved her and protected her and been her big sister. But after she'd disappeared, it was as if Clare hadn't existed. Everything was always about Lynnie. And Clare had just wanted her parents to realize that although her sister was gone, *she* was still there.

Shara, on the other hand, had always had all of Clare's attention. What she didn't have was a father. She'd been a precocious child, constantly testing her boundaries. Sometimes Clare just got weary of being a watchdog. But yet wasn't that what parents were supposed to do?

After taking a deep breath for patience then putting her chin-length brown hair behind her ears, she reached out and took the blouse from Shara's hands. It really wasn't a blouse, just a stretch lace concoction that *her* daughter wasn't going to be caught dead in. "If you wear this out on the street, you'll get arrested. What did you buy to go with it?" She meant to keep her tone curious but it sounded judgmental anyway.

Shara produced a pair of black leather shorts that Clare suspected would fit too snugly.

"The outfit goes back. It's not appropriate for school. It's not appropriate to wear to the mall. It's not appropriate to be caught dusting the house in. What were you thinking?"

"I'm thinking there are a few boys who would think I'm hot."

Counting to ten had never been a strategy that worked well for Clare, especially when her daughter was deliberately trying to push her buttons. But she tried it again, nonetheless, not meeting with any more success than she'd achieved the last time. She prayed for patience, or wisdom or anything that would help deal with her daughter.

Finally, in a friendly tone she asked, "Care to give me their names? Maybe I can do background checks."

Shara studied her mother, trying to decide if she was joking or serious. "Brad said he likes me in black."

"Brad doesn't need to like you in anything. He's a senior. You're a sophomore. We've talked about this,

Shara. He has a reputation and I don't want him giving *you* a reputation."

"You are wound *so* tight," Shara mumbled.

Before Clare could deal with *that* assessment, the telephone rang. She glanced at it, thought about letting it ring, letting the answering machine take over. But maybe both she and her daughter needed a few minutes to cool down. She saw from the Caller ID that it was her mom's home number. This would probably be a short conversation. They never had much to say to each other.

Clare watched Shara take the new outfit and her other bags to her room. "They go back," Clare called after her.

Her daughter didn't bother to reply.

Clare greeted her mom with a chipper "hello," wondering what she was going to put together for supper. As an X-ray technician at the hospital, she usually arrived home after Shara. Today, however, Shara had asked her if she could stop at the mall for an hour or so after school and Clare had agreed. It looked as if they'd both be taking a trip after supper to return Shara's purchases. Maybe they should just leave now and grab pizza there. The mall on an October Friday night would be busy.

"Clare?"

The tiny crack in her mother's voice made Clare pull in a breath. "What's wrong? Has something happened to Dad?"

Although her father and mother had divorced two years after Lynnie had disappeared, Clare had desperately tried to hold onto bonds with both of them.

"I haven't heard from your father in weeks. The last time I saw him was at the picnic you had Labor Day weekend."

It was really strange. Her parents had once had a good marriage until Lynnie was taken. Now they were awkward together whenever they had to be in the same room. Clare always felt as if she were the cause of that awkwardness, always felt as if she should do something to make it all better, always felt as if she was the neutral territory in the middle of a decades-old war.

After a short pause, her mother explained, "Detective Grove called me. He already spoke to your father."

Clare's heart skipped a beat. "Detective Grove?" The picture of a tall lean man in a rumpled suit flashed in her mind—the man who had taken over Lynnie's investigation after the patrol officers' first visit.

"Do you remember him?" her mother asked gently—too gently—and Clare had a shivery premonition of what could be coming.

"Didn't he retire?" she asked her mom, her heart racing now.

"Yes, he did. But he's not really keen on retirement and he's been...working a few cold cases." Her mother's voice was edgier than usual and a little wobbly, too.

"What are you trying to tell me, Mom?" Clare's hands became sweaty as she thought about all the possibilities. Lynnie's face at three and a half was still so vivid in her mind—the face they'd used on posters...the face she'd envisioned floating in a river...the face on the body in nightmares that had been buried in a ditch. The *not* knowing had always been worse than knowing. The <u>not</u>

knowing is what had torn them all apart. Clare really believed that if the police had found Lynnie's body somewhere, maybe they could have gone on as a family.

Maybe.

"He wants to meet with us tomorrow morning. You, me and your dad. He thinks he has a lead."

Clare's throat went desert dry. Even though she'd only been five, she remembered the hope that had filled her parents' faces whenever a new lead had been phoned in, whenever the police had gotten a tip from an informer on the street, whenever there was a chance that Lynnie might have been spotted. She also remembered the expression on their faces when all those hopes had been dashed and one day had turned into the next without teaching them anything new.

Except that they were losing each other, hour by hour, day by day, week by week.

"What kind of lead?" Clare asked, trying to control the shakiness in her voice.

"He wouldn't tell me over the phone. He's working out of his home, so I offered the use of my office at *Yesteryear*. Can you be there tomorrow at ten?"

Her father wouldn't like meeting at her mother's shop. Now and then he'd complained to Clare that her mother was lost in the past. He didn't like the mustiness of the store or what the old furniture represented—a history that couldn't be changed...a child who would never come home. Her mother didn't see it that way at all. Her mother liked to relive every memory she had. She wrapped herself in the reminiscence of what she told Clare were the happiest years of her life. More than that, *Yesteryear* had given her a reason to get up each day, a reason to search for old furniture if not for her daughter, though Clare suspected she still looked for Lynnie everywhere she went.

Trying to prepare herself for the meeting, she shored up her courage and asked, "Did Detective Grove say whether this lead means Lynnie's alive or dead?"

A sharp intake of breath met her question and then her mom answered, "He didn't say, and I didn't ask. I still have hope, Clare. I always have."

Yes, her mother had held onto the hope that Lynnie was still alive, that some misguided woman had taken her and raised her for her own. But a misguided woman didn't steal a child from someone's house in the middle of the night.

False hope was worse than no hope at all. Clare and her dad understood each other on that one point, at least.

"I'll be there tomorrow, Mom, but please don't—" She wasn't sure how to say it.

"Please don't believe in the best rather than the worst? Oh, Clare. Maybe as you get older you'll learn that believing in the best is the only way to get through some days. I'll see you in the morning, honey."

Clare and her mother weren't on the same wavelength...would never be on the same wavelength. Just like her and Shara?

She said goodbye, hung up the phone and went to her daughter's room. Arguing with Shara would postpone thinking about the meeting tomorrow morning...a meeting that could shake up all of their lives once more.

ABOUT THE AUTHOR
Karen Rose Smith

Award-winning author Karen Rose Smith was born in Pennsylvania. Although she was an only child, she remembers the bonds of an extended family. Since her father came from a family of ten and her mother, a family of seven, there were always aunts, uncles and cousins visiting on weekends. Family is a strong theme in her books and she suspects her childhood memories are the reason.

In college, Karen began writing poetry and also met her husband to be. They both began married life as teachers, but when their son was born, Karen decided to try her hand at a home-decorating business. She returned to teaching for a while but changes in her life led her to writing romance fiction. Now she writes romances and mysteries full time. She has sold over 80 novels since 1991.

Presently, she is hard at work on a series for Harlequin Special Edition as well as the Caprice De Luca home stager mystery series for Kensington Books. When she isn't writing, she cares for three rescue cats, gardens, and cooks. Married to her college sweetheart since 1971, believing in the power of love and commitment, she envisions herself writing relationship novels, both romance and mystery, for a long time to come!

For more about Karen and her latest releases, visit her websites at www.karenrosesmith.com and www.karenrose smithmysteries.com. To keep in touch day to day, follow Karen at Facebook, on Twitter, on her Cats, Roses...and Books! blog and her IN TOUCH with Karen Rose Smith e-zine.